I dedicate this book to my mother.

Mom, you have graciously read all the stories I've written, helping correct mistakes while offering suggestions. You have been an encouragement to me along the way, all the while hoping for greater things to come. Mom, you are my biggest fan.

I love you!

Her teachings are filled with wisdom and kindness as loving instruction pours from her lips.
Proverbs 31:26

A PATRIOT'S DREAM

CHRIS DAVIS

Copyright © 2023 Chris Davis

All rights reserved. No part of this book may be reproduced in any form or by any electronic or mechanical means, including information storage and retrieval systems, without permission in writing from the copyright holder, except by reviewers, who may quote brief passages in a review.

ISBN: 979-8-9891536-0-2

Printed by Athens Printing Company
Athens, GA USA

Edited by MK Editing

Formatted by Chris Davis
Cover design by Chris Davis

www.chrisdavisauthor.net

— A PATRIOT'S DREAM —

The Dream

"A candle loses nothing when it lights another candle."
Thomas Jefferson

The warm sun beamed down on Caroline's face while a cool breeze blew through her red hair. She stood atop a bluff overlooking a harbor full of ships, the likes of which she had never before seen. Most looked to be made of metal, not wood, and had no sails.

As she studied the scene below, the feeling of heaviness Caroline had lived under for much of her life suddenly felt as if it had been lifted from her shoulders.

"*Freedom,*" she whispered to herself without thinking. "It feels like freedom."

But it was more than just a feeling. The freedom she now experienced was tangible and couldn't be hidden or explained away. While Caroline soaked in the moment, something above her whipped around in the wind, vying for her attention. She slowly raised her head and gasped.

"One, two, three. . ." Caroline began counting the white stars within the blue square of the star-spangled banner that fluttered in the wind. "Fifty stars!" Her eyes narrowed. "Fifty colonies?"

Now Caroline knew she was dreaming but what a dream this was. Clear, vivid, and filled with hope. Something within her spirit, however, declared this was much more than just a dream. Perhaps, it was the very future she saw. *Yes, that's it! The future!*

"We did it!" Her eyes filled with tears, something that seldom happened. "We won the war!"

Victory lay ahead for her people—if only they could stay the course and not give up.

The beautiful banner of red, white, and blue blowing in the wind began to fade as the dream came to an end, but not Caroline's hope. It was growing and strengthening into a blazing fire within her heart.

— A PATRIOT'S DREAM —

Pennsylvania
September 1777

"The fate of unborn millions will now depend, under God, on the courage and conduct of this army. We have, therefore, to resolve to conquer or die."
George Washington

The wagon jostled Caroline, waking her from a short nap as they entered the military encampment. The sun had just dipped below the horizon as dusk approached.

"I can't believe I fell asleep," Caroline muttered as she got on her knees and peered ahead. "Are we there?"

"That we are," her father replied without glancing back as he pulled on the reins, bringing the horses to a stop.

Caroline and her father had just fled Philadelphia as the British Army marched into the city and captured it, but escaping had not been without a fight. She glanced down at two wounded soldiers who had come with her father to get Caroline out of the city.

Little of anything seemed to be going in America's favor as the war with Britain raged on. Now the capital of the American colonies had been captured by the Redcoats, and Congress had fled for their lives. Maybe God's grace for their independence had all been used up.

The looks on the faces of many soldiers at the encampment couldn't hide the fear and hopelessness that all may be lost.

Caroline grabbed her rifle and jumped down from the back of the wagon as her father walked around.

"We have wounded!" her father yelled and lowered the tailgate.

Several soldiers ran over and began helping the two wounded men out of the wagon.

Caroline's father stepped behind her and put his hands on her shoulders. "So thankful we got you out when we did. I can't lose you too."

She closed her eyes, pushing away the sorrow from six months ago when the British killed her mother and brother. Even after all this time, it still didn't seem possible that they were gone.

"Now, I've got to find somewhere for you to stay. I'm going to inquire with Aunt Mildred in North Carolina and see if she would be willing to take you in for a season."

"Mama always said Aunt Mildred was loyal to the king." Caroline shook her head. "I can't go live with—"

"Her views are changing—slowly." Her father didn't sound very confident. "Nonetheless, it's safer with her."

"Papa." Caroline turned around. "Let me stay with you from here on out. I'm good with a rifle and hate the Brits as much as anyone. Why I know I shot at least two Redcoats on the way out of—"

"Caroline." Her father's voice rose. He paused while his expression quickly softened. "You're all I have left, and things are not boding well for our side. Winter will soon be upon us and—"

"Papa, I want to stay with—"

"There's nothing out here but pain and death, Caroline!" Her father's voice rose again.

"I'm not afraid." She set her jaw, unwilling to give in. "I want to fight, Papa. I owe that to Mama and Paul."

"Caroline—" Her father shook his head and looked away as his eyes began to fill. His heart had been broken by their deaths. Now he appeared to hold on too tightly to Caroline, trying to keep her safe at all costs. But there were few places to hide from the war. Caroline was a fighter, not a coward who ran off to a haven to save her own neck while others sacrificed theirs.

Her father sighed out loud. "For now, you'll stay by my side until other arrangements can be made. But you must do exactly as I tell you—"

"Thank you, Papa." Caroline put her rifle down and wrapped her arms around him. "I'll make you proud."

"I already am." He squeezed her. "Come on. Let's get situated for the night."

— A PATRIOT'S DREAM —

As they passed by a makeshift flagpole made from a small tree stripped of its branches, Caroline glanced up, watching the tattered flag with thirteen stars slowly dance in the evening breeze. She gasped and stopped as *the dream* shot to the forefront of her mind.

"What is it?" Her father's brows grew tight.

"A dream. No, more than a dream," she whispered as the memory of the flag of fifty stars grew stronger. "Papa—we're going to win this war."

"Let us hope so. Only the good Lord above knows for sure."

"Yes, He does, and now I do too." A smile grew on her face as she stared at the flag.

Her father put his arm on her shoulder. "Come on. Let's go."

****

Caroline stepped outside the tent she and her father shared and into the cool darkness. Several torches glowed in the encampment as soldiers moved about in preparation for battle. It had been a long week since Caroline joined her father, and she had grown restless. Today, that would change.

After observing the activity of the British troops, General Washington felt now was the time to strike. At dawn, a battle would be waged to take back Philadelphia.

Caroline's father told her about the battle plan, one in which the Americans would break up into regiments and attack the British encampment outside of Philadelphia from four directions.

Her father stepped out of the tent with his rifle in hand. "Keep us in your prayers today." He looked around as other soldiers in his regiment gathered nearby. "If for some reason the battle should come back this way, I want you to leave quickly with the others and—"

"Papa, I'm not running away—"

"You'll do as you're told, Caroline!" Her father's face firmed.

She sighed and folded her arms but said nothing more. There was no way Caroline could make a promise to her father that she couldn't keep, so silence was her best ally.

After kissing Caroline goodbye, her father left with the regiment under General Nathan Greene's command. When he was almost out of sight, Caroline slipped back into their tent and opened a bag. She carefully pulled out a blue tricorne hat and a makeshift uniform she had swiped from the supplies the day before and altered for herself with needle and thread.

"Sorry, Papa. I can't sit by and do nothing," Caroline whispered as she quickly pinned up her long, red hair and got dressed.

Once she had buckled her belt, Caroline grabbed her rifle and stepped out of the tent, looking across the encampment for General Sullivan's regiment whom she would secretly join in battle. Few within his army had seen or knew of her. Hopefully, Caroline could pass for a young-looking seventeen-year-old boy, although she knew that may be a stretch.

"Oh, no! They've already left the camp. I'm late!" Caroline held her hat and ran in the moonlight to catch up.

Her heart raced while butterflies filled her stomach. This wasn't the first time Caroline had been in a fight. Six months ago, she had briefly fought the British while defending her home. On that dark day, her mama and brother died at the hands of the Redcoats.

This day, however, she considered herself a soldier in the Continental Army, ready to exact her revenge for their deaths and push the British out of Philadelphia.

Her father said morale was low among the Americans as most questioned whether they could defeat the well-armed British troops. But Caroline had seen evidence of their victory. The flag of fifty stars in her night vision didn't lie. God must have shown it to her because He was on their side.

"That has to be the reason," she whispered.

As Caroline approached the soldiers under General Sullivan's command, she slipped in on the outside of the long column of troops marching toward Germantown.

A soldier beside her with sandy blond hair and slightly boyish features looked over and frowned. "You're late!" he whispered. "Best be glad Sullivan didn't see that."

Caroline nodded but said nothing, hoping he wouldn't look too closely and realize she wasn't a part of the army. Right now, the darkness would help conceal that fact.

General Sullivan rode his horse out in front of the troops as they moved across the Pennsylvanian landscape toward their enemy. As they marched, Caroline's thoughts turned to her father, wondering if she would encounter him on the battlefield when all four columns of Washington's army converged on the British. Hopefully, she could avoid being seen by him and make it back to camp to change out of the uniform before he arrived.

As the sun broke on the eastern horizon, Sullivan's army approached the center of the British encampment amidst the foggy terrain. Upon seeing the Americans, the unprepared British soldiers scurried to get into battle formation.

"We've caught them by surprise!" the young man beside Caroline whispered out loud with a smirk on his face.

Just then, General Sullivan rode off to the side of the long column of his troops and raised his sword. "Make ready!"

At his command, Caroline and the rest of the soldiers slid their rifles off their shoulders and held them upright while pulling back their firing hammers.

"Present!" The general's voice filled the air.

Caroline lowered the rifle and fixed the end of the barrel on a Redcoat running out of his tent.

"Fire!" Sullivan yelled.

She pulled the trigger, and the black powder ignited while a small cloud of white smoke shot up into the air. The British soldier within her sight grabbed his chest and fell to the ground.

"That's for Mama," she muttered under her breath.

"Nice shot!" The soldier beside Caroline began reloading his rifle. "Don't recall seeing you before. The name's Nathan."

"I'm Carol—" Caroline hesitated. "Uh, Cody," she replied in a slightly deeper voice.

Exhilaration pumped through Caroline's veins as she pulled out a musket cartridge from the leather pouch on her belt and tore off the end of the paper tube with her teeth. Carefully, she poured some of the black powder into the priming pan of the rifle before pouring the remaining powder and musket ball down the barrel. After packing it down with the ramrod, Caroline took aim again and fired. Another Redcoat fell to the ground.

"And that's for Paul," she spoke through clenched teeth.

With the British caught off guard and in disarray, General Sullivan signaled his troops to move ahead. "Forward march!"

"We've got them on the run now!" Nathan exclaimed as they quickened their pace.

Part of the British Army briskly retreated into the foggy woods. If the other three columns of the American Army were having the same success that General Sullivan's troops were, then maybe they could retake Philadelphia by nightfall.

A two-story house made of stone faintly appeared within the fog as Sullivan's army continued their pursuit. Caroline could just make out the British fleeing past the house. The Americans' pace quickened.

— A PATRIOT'S DREAM —

Suddenly, Redcoats appeared in all the windows of the mansion and opened fire. Several of the unsuspecting soldiers of the Continental Army fell.

"Those sly little buggers." Nathan shot at the house, shattering a section of a second-story window but missing the enemy. "This makes it a trite bit harder taking them out."

The British darted in and out of the windows while taking shots at the Americans. Caroline's unit stayed to fight the enemy within the house while another section of General Sullivan's troops moved out into the fog to pursue the fleeing British.

Caroline took aim and waited until a Redcoat appeared and then opened fire. The musket ball hit a soldier in the head, and he stumbled forward, falling out the window to the ground.

"Say, you really are a good shot." Nathan slid the ramrod back into his rifle after reloading.

"My father was a great teacher," Caroline replied in a deeper voice.

As the fighting continued, the battle to subdue the stone mansion appeared to be failing. More of the American troops fell, their bodies littering the land around the house. Victory which once seemed to be within reach was quickly fading.

"I'm down to three shots left." Nathan reloaded. "How about you?"

Caroline glanced in her musket pouch. "Four."

"I don't think this strategy is working very well." Nathan crouched down as he reloaded. He glanced past the house into the fog. "We can't maintain a fight without more ammunition. And where's the rest of our regiment—"

A cannon blast came from the east, exploding nearby while more British troops appeared to be closing in. The battle thickened, sending the Americans into disarray as they tried to regroup.

Another soldier beside Caroline was shot by the British and stumbled into her, knocking her down as he held his bloody throat, gasping for air. Caroline cringed, wanting to help him, but there was nothing she could do. The man's eyes slowly closed, and he became still. Caroline's tears rose as she stared at him. This man could just have easily been her father.

"Fall back!" A nearby officer gave the command to the Continental Army. "Retreat!"

"Come on!" Nathan helped push the dead man off Caroline. "Let's go!"

As she stood, a shot whizzed through the air, knocking Caroline's hat off her head. Dazed, she staggered over, feeling slightly disoriented as she snatched her hat from the ground. She quickly put it back on her head lest Nathan see her pinned-up hair.

Nathan picked Caroline's rifle up. "Don't forget this—" His eyes widened when he looked over at her. "Cody, you've been hit."

Caroline placed her hand on the right side of her forehead in disbelief as a stinging pain set in. She pulled her hand away and glanced down at the blood covering it. A wave of dizziness washed over her, and she stumbled, nearly falling down.

Nathan swung his rifle over his shoulder and grabbed Caroline's arm to steady her. "I've got you, Cody. Come on, let's get out of here."

What was left of Caroline's unit retreated westward into the fog as the British pursued. She pressed a handkerchief against her head while they quickly moved away from the battle. Slowly, the dizziness passed, and the shock of being hit by a musket ball began to ease. The wound had caused unwanted attention to herself. Despite this, Caroline was thankful to have someone like Nathan assist her after becoming dazed.

"I feel a little better." Caroline pulled against Nathan's hold. "You can let go now."

"Glad to hear it. That was close."

Gunfire continued from behind in the shroud of fog as another of the American columns appeared to engage the British. She prayed silently for her father's protection, not knowing where he was.

The bleeding finally slowed, much to Caroline's relief. This was the part of going into battle she would have to get used to. At any moment during combat, death could come. She would have to be more vigilant and not let her guard down for a second.

Part of Sullivan's army returned to camp in the late afternoon, tired and feeling defeated. The wounded soldiers were instructed to receive medical attention.

Caroline's wound only seemed to complicate matters. She would have to somehow hide it from her father. Maybe when she let her hair down, it would cover it.

"No, that won't work," Caroline grunted in frustration as she headed toward her tent. "He'd still see it. I'll have to come up with some kind of excuse, like tripping and falling against a tree. Don't know if he'll believe—"

"Cody!" Nathan yelled as he headed her way.

She ignored him, not wanting to talk. Caroline had to get cleaned up before her father arrived.

Nathan grabbed her arm. "Where are you going? You need to get that wound checked."

Caroline shook her head. "No, I'm fine."

"That's not a request. All soldiers hurt in battle must get looked after." Nathan stood in front of her.

She looked down. Though Caroline wore her hair up and kept a plain complexion on her face, her features might still give her away as a girl if too closely examined. And girls were not allowed to fight in Washington's Army.

But refusing to obey orders would only draw more attention to herself. This had become more complicated than Caroline had planned. Now she wished she had never met Nathan. He was ruining everything.

Caroline sighed in frustration. "Fine."

Moments later, Caroline stood in line to see one of the doctors. She glanced over toward the woods as General Greene's troops slowly made their way into camp. Anxiety rose within her. Caroline needed to hurry and get cleaned up and changed or there would be hell to pay. But Nathan stood to the side, watching her like a hawk. Running off wasn't an option.

"God, I hate that boy," she whispered through clenched teeth while glancing at Nathan.

"Next." A doctor motioned her over. "What's your name?"

"Cody Johnson." Caroline stepped closer and removed the bloodied handkerchief from her head. She shifted her hat upward just enough so he could examine the wound.

"I'm Doctor Richardson." The man's eyes narrowed as he studied Caroline's forehead. "Well, Cody, it looks like a surface wound. Lucky for you. Another inch or so to the left, and you'd be dead."

As the doctor began to clean the wound, he appeared to study her. "How old are you, Cody?"

"Uh, I'm seventeen," Caroline replied in a deeper voice.

"Seventeen?" The doctor's lips scrunched together. "Look young for your age." He glanced over at Nathan who stood off to the side. "How old are you, son?"

"Seventeen, sir."

The doctor's piercing gaze returned to Caroline, making her feel even more uncomfortable.

If only that stupid boy had just minded his own business. Caroline fumed.

"I'd be surprised if you're a day over fifteen," the doctor mumbled. "But I suppose we need all the help we can get."

When he tried to remove Caroline's hat, she quickly pressed her hand against it.

"I can't bandage your head with your hat on, Cody. Please, remove it."

"Are you sure you can't just wrap the—"

"Cody, remove your hat!" The doctor yelled. "There are others waiting for medical attention."

Reluctantly, Caroline complied. As she took the hat off, a strand of her long red hair flopped down from her bun.

The doctor's brows furrowed while a look of anger washed over his face. "War is no place for little girls!"

"I'm not a little girl!" Caroline fired back. "I'll be fifteen next month!"

Nathan's eyes widened in disbelief as did several of the men waiting in line. Everything was coming unraveled. Now, she *loathed* that stupid boy.

"It matters not when your birthday is!" The doctor growled. "You shouldn't be out here in the first place! Are your parents encamped here, or did you run away from home?"

"My father is in General Greene's column." Caroline's voice fell as the fear of facing her father grew.

"What's his name?" Doctor Richardson demanded.

"William Johnson," Caroline whispered while her gaze dropped to the ground, feeling sick to her stomach.

The doctor glanced up as General Greene's troops moved across the encampment. He looked over at Nathan. "Go find her father."

"Yes, sir."

One ill-timed shot in the head had undone everything. Now Caroline felt small and humiliated. But that didn't seem right or fair. If she was able, why shouldn't she be allowed to fight for the same cause her father did—as did every man in this army?

"My daughter is close to your age." A frown remained on the doctor's face as he bandaged Caroline's head. "There's no way in hell I'd have her out here fighting in battle."

Caroline bit her tongue to avoid saying something she'd regret.

Just then, her father walked up with Nathan beside him. "What in God's name is going on?"

"I was about to ask you the same thing." The doctor glanced over. "What kind of father sends his young daughter out into battle?"

"Battle?" An angry expression grew on her father's face.

"Yes." Doctor Richardson nodded. "She barely escaped with her life."

"Caroline—I told you to stay put." Her father spoke through clenched teeth.

The doctor wiped his hands on a rag as he looked over at Caroline's father. "See to it that she stays with her mother during the battles and not—"

"Mama's dead!" Caroline yelled as her fiery gaze connected with Doctor Richardson. "The British killed her. And there's no way in hell that I'm going to sit by and do nothing about it—"

"Caroline! Watch your tongue!" Her father's voice rose.

"I'm sorry, Papa. I mean no disrespect." She put her hat back on her bandaged head. "I'm here to fight for our freedom just like you, and I can do it."

"I will say that she's a good shot." Nathan looked to be holding back a smile. "Better than most. Don't think she missed once today."

"That's not the point." Her father glared at Nathan. "She shouldn't be out there to begin with!"

Nathan shrugged. "I'm just reporting what I saw. She's good with a rifle."

Her father walked over and snatched Caroline by the arm. "Come with me!"

As the two marched toward their tent, Caroline wondered if he would spank her. It had been quite some time since she had required such discipline. Its effects wouldn't be the same as when she was a little girl.

"Sit down!" he yelled after they stepped inside the tent. "What in God's name were you thinking?"

Caroline said nothing, allowing her father to continue ranting about his concerns and disappointments. After finishing, he sat down on his cot as tears rose in his eyes.

"I love you too much, little one, to see you die at the hands of the British. You're all I have left."

"I love you too, Papa." Her gaze trailed off to the dirt floor as she collected her thoughts. "But I feel like I'm being smothered by your love."

"What?"

"I feel like you're holding on so tight to me that I can't breathe—I can't live." Her eyes reconnected with his. "Papa—you can't protect me from the world."

A sob leaped from his throat, and he looked away. He must know this was the truth.

She stepped over and sat beside him. "I don't want to hurt you, Papa. Ever since Mama and Paul died, I've felt a fire burning inside me. I want to fight for freedom like you and everyone else. I know we can win—*will* win."

He put his arm around her and pulled her close. "I never thought when I held you in my arms as a little nugget of joy, that one day we would be faced with such darkness. I'd always dreamed of a happy family growing old together in love. Mama and I dreamed of grandchildren and—" His voice broke.

Caroline began crying with him. The dream of happiness they once held onto had been stolen—burned up by the war. Now, they fought, hoping to live long enough to see freedom. Without it, there could never be true happiness again.

****

Caroline sat around a campfire at night with her father, Nathan, and several other soldiers at the encampment. Over the last couple of days, news had gotten around about a girl who bravely fought against the British at Germantown with deadly accuracy.

That news was met with mixed views. Some of the soldiers were inspired while others were offended. In the end, Caroline was surprisingly given permission by General Sullivan to continue serving in Washington's Army. Caroline's father had reluctantly and tearfully given his blessing.

With this all out in the open, Caroline felt a weight lifted off her shoulders. There would be no more sneaking around, lowering her voice, or using a fake name. Now she could focus on fighting for freedom.

But the war with Great Britain continued to go downhill for the Americans. Germantown was but another defeat at the hands of the British. General Sullivan's column had been the only one to fully engage the Redcoats and briefly pushed them back. Fog and bad timing had confused the other three American columns, leading them to fire upon one another by mistake.

"This feels hopeless," one of the soldiers around the fire muttered. "How are we supposed to fight against the British Empire and win? I know I'm not the only one who feels this way."

Nathan looked over at the man. "You want to live under King George's foot all your life?"

"At least we'd be alive. I don't—" The soldier hesitated and glanced over his shoulder as if concerned about being overheard. "I don't think our leadership knows what they're doing—if you get my meaning."

— A PATRIOT'S DREAM —

"Even if they did, there's no way we can win." Franklin, another pessimistic soldier, shook his head. "The king will just keep sending more Redcoats—"

"We *will* win this war." Caroline pushed her way into the conversation. "We *will* defeat the Redcoats."

"Blind faith of the young." A soldier spat on the ground. "Give it a few months, and you'll change your tune."

"No, I won't." Caroline shook her head. "I've seen it."

"Seen what?" Franklin's eyes narrowed.

Caroline's father placed his hand on hers as if encouraging her to remain silent. When she had shared *the dream* with him earlier, he told Caroline to keep it to herself. These battle-hardened men might just as well mock her than believe in *the dream*. That would only bring about pain.

But Caroline couldn't keep silent.

"I saw our flag with fifty stars on it. God showed it to me in a dream," Caroline blurted out. "We *will* win this war and be free of the British forever. We just can't give up."

"God gave you a dream?" Franklin burst into laughter. "Told you that we'd win the war?"

"Fifty stars! And what bottle have you been drinking from, little missy?" A soldier beside Franklin mocked her before joining in the laughter.

"No offense." Another of their comrades glanced over at Caroline and her father with a tired expression. "But that was just a dream. I wish it could be more than that, but what we're facing is reality."

"Fifty stars." Franklin slapped his knee while his mocking laughter grew.

Caroline jumped to her feet and stormed off toward the edge of the woods before stopping. "I saw what I saw," she muttered to herself as she looked up into the starry night sky, wondering if God had been listening to the conversation by the fire. "I *know* You showed it to me. It felt too real to be —"

"Cody—uh, Caroline." Nathan approached.

"I don't want to hear it from you either!" Caroline yelled and folded her arms, wishing this boy would go to another bonfire way across the camp, or, better yet, would go get lost in the woods. If Caroline never saw him again, she'd be better for it.

Nathan stopped beside her. "You've got me intrigued. I want to hear more about the dream."

She rolled her eyes and looked at him suspiciously.

"Seriously, I really do."

Caroline sighed, not sure she believed him.

"Look, don't pay those blokes any attention. They've seen more battles than we have and are just cynical. Honestly, I can't blame them." He looked up into the sky. "Right now, we could all use a bit of hope."

Caroline's anger toward him eased. Maybe Nathan wasn't like the others, and maybe he wasn't half as bad as she believed him to be. The truth was, Nathan had only been trying to help her after she got wounded, not make her life miserable.

"Okay, but you better not laugh!" Caroline pointed her finger at him. "I mean it."

"Fair enough." He nodded.

— A PATRIOT'S DREAM —

She took a deep breath and exhaled. "Well, I saw a harbor, only it was very large, and the ships weren't like anything I've seen before. Then I heard something and looked up. Fluttering in the wind above me was one of the most beautiful things I've ever seen. The red, white, and blue flag appeared strong and unblemished. Right after I counted the fifty stars, *the dream* ended." Caroline's gaze returned to the sky. "In my heart, I just know it was real. It was from God."

"I believe you."

"You do?" Her brows rose.

He nodded. "I, too, believe in my heart that we are destined to win this war. The British control far too much in this world. There must be somewhere on this earth where one can be free, and I believe this land is it." Nathan glanced over at Caroline. "It must be."

Warmth grew within Caroline's heart as she listened. Nathan seemed to understand. Maybe they weren't too different after all.

"Don't let those old buggers tame you, Caroline." A smile rose on Nathan's face. "You just keep on dreaming. It *will* come to pass one day. I just know it."

— A PATRIOT'S DREAM —

— A PATRIOT'S DREAM —

Pennsylvania
December 1777

"The tree of liberty must be refreshed from time to time with the blood of patriots and tyrants."
Thomas Jefferson

Caroline stepped out of her tent in the bright moonlight and yawned; her warm breath drifted up into the cold air before dissipating. For the last three months, she had been among the soldiers, learning more about the art of war and the discipline of being in the army.

She and her comrades had moved to the new encampment a few weeks ago, and now there was talk of General Washington taking the army to Valley Forge. But that was many miles farther west of Philadelphia. In

— A PATRIOT'S DREAM —

Caroline's mind, taking back their capital should be a priority.

After relieving herself in the woods, Caroline headed back to her tent. Just then, several cannon blasts went off in the distance. Were those shots to alert the Continental Army, or were they from the enemy?

Nathan ran over. "General Howe's Army's been spotted coming in from the east. Get dressed and grab your rifle."

Caroline ducked back into her tent. "Papa." She shook him from a deep sleep. "The British are coming our way."

"What?" He sat up and rubbed his eyes. "In the middle of the night?"

"It appears so."

Moments later, Caroline and her father were dressed and moved out to their designated assignments. But the orders given to her regiment were not what she expected.

"Build more campfires?" Caroline helped drag branches from the woods. "Why are we wasting time with this?"

"Right now, it looks like we're outnumbered by the British." Nathan propped up the wood within a circular pit. "General Washington gave orders to build more campfires and try to deceive General Howe into believing there are more of us than there really are."

"His army is camped just over the hill," another soldier added. "I hope this works."

Nathan held a torch to the dried leaves and twigs. The flames quickly grew into a roaring fire. Many other campfires also burned, lighting up the hillside. Now Caroline and her comrades waited with their rifles in hand.

The Redcoats, however, never came that night.

As the sun rose the following day, the British began firing their cannons, though they appeared to be too far away to hit the American encampment. Gunfire from smaller skirmishes echoed from all directions, still, Caroline and Nathan stood around with their contingent, waiting.

By the following morning, things had changed. Part of General Howe's forces were moving in from the east, trying to flank the Continental Army and reach their encampment.

"Move out!" The commanding officer gave the order to the regiment Caroline and Nathan had been assigned to.

"Finally." She placed her rifle over her shoulder and marched eastward. "I *hate* waiting around."

"Good thing you're not our strategist," Nathan jested.

"I suppose." Caroline briefly smirked. "But I would love nothing more than to put a shot in General Howe's head."

Nathan raised an eyebrow. "Got your eyes set on revenge?"

She nodded. "His army is the one who killed Mama and Paul."

"Oh, I see."

"My mother and brother weren't even armed. They were just trying to get out of harm's way. Both were shot in the back."

"How'd you avoid getting killed?"

"After briefly fighting the British, my uncle and I escaped. He's currently serving in Benedict Arnold's forces. Papa was stationed with Washington's army when this happened."

"Oh, I see. So, that's when your father came back and moved you to Philadelphia?"

"Yes." Caroline sighed. "Now, I'm homeless."

"Well, I, for one, am thankful the British didn't end your life." Nathan smiled.

Caroline returned the smile, glad to have Nathan as a friend to face the uncertainties of life with. He would watch her back, and she would watch his.

As Caroline's regiment entered a dense forest, an uneasiness washed over her. It seemed too quiet. She slid her rifle off her shoulder and held it in both hands as her gaze narrowed ahead.

Suddenly, gunshots rang out, and the bark of the tree beside Caroline splintered.

"Take cover!" an officer yelled as the British began firing at them.

Caroline jumped behind a tree, took a deep breath, and exhaled. "That was close. Be careful, Caroline. Don't get yourself killed," she mumbled.

From the number of shots fired, it appeared her contingent was outnumbered by the British.

"Okay, here we go," Caroline whispered to herself and swung her rifle from around a tree, eyeing anything red.

There!

A British soldier stepped out some twenty yards away with his barrel fixed on her. However, Caroline fired first, hitting the man in the shoulder. She quickly stepped back behind the tree as gunshots pelted the bark.

"I believe the trees are going to get the worst of it in this battle," Nathan said as he took aim and fired.

"Probably." Caroline packed down the black powder with her ramrod. "Better a tree than my flesh."

As the battle continued, the British slowly inched closer, shifting from tree to tree, though the Americans held their position. The smokey haze of spent black powder grew thicker throughout the forest, making it more challenging to see clearly.

A comrade to her right fell to the ground, moaning in pain from a leg wound.

"Stay down!" Nathan yelled as he reloaded his rifle. "And put pressure on the wound."

The battle raged on in a stalemate. The main goal of Caroline's regiment, however, was to keep the British from advancing toward the American encampment.

Caroline pulled out another musket cartridge from her pouch. "I'm down to three shots left." She quickly poured the black powder and ball down into the barrel.

"I've got four." Nathan stepped out and fired. "It doesn't look like we have any reinforcements coming to our aid. Maybe the British will get bored and leave."

"If only it were that easy." Caroline pressed her back against the tree after reloading.

When she stepped out to fire, she noticed British reinforcements moving in. "Oh, no! More Redcoats." She slipped back behind the tree as fear rose within her. "They're going to flank us, and we're almost out of ammunition."

Caroline glanced over at Nathan. "Should we retreat?"

"Not without orders."

"But how are we going to fight?" She shook her head. "Throwing rocks won't work."

Nathan pulled out another packet from his pouch and looked at it. "We'll just hold our fire until they get closer."

That didn't seem like very good strategy. Death was knocking at the door. This skirmish had a similar feeling to the battle at Germantown in the sense that they were outnumbered and running out of ammunition. If they left now, they could live to fight another day.

Caroline peered around the tree as the Redcoat reinforcements moved closer. "Nathan, I think—"

"Pull back!" an officer nearby yelled. "Pull back!"

"Thank, God," she muttered.

"Cover me, Caroline, while I help Charles." Nathan slung his rifle around his shoulder and got low, crawling over to their wounded comrade.

Caroline stepped out eyeing a redcoat drawing closer to their position and fired. "Got you," she mumbled as the enemy soldier fell.

Before the British could cut them off, the Americans quickly retreated from the hazy woods, dodging from tree to tree until they were out of the forest. The British, however, did not pursue them. A small blessing within the scope of the entire war.

The following day, it was reported that General Howe's troops were heading back to Philadelphia. Though the reasoning for the British move eluded Caroline, she was thankful just the same. She'd prefer that the Continental

Army fight on their own terms. Maybe they could regroup within a week or two and try once more to reclaim the capital before winter set in.

A couple of days later, however, new orders came down from General Washington.

"This is so disappointing!" Caroline griped as she and her father packed up their tent and belongings. "I was hoping for one more opportunity to attack the British and take back Philadelphia."

"That will have to wait until the spring." Her father tied his pack tight. "For now, we have an eight-day trek to Valley Forge."

"We'll be there all winter?" Caroline glanced over at him.

Her father nodded. "Until early April or May, I surmise."

Caroline looked toward the east once more before they headed out. If only spring would come soon.

****

The red, white, and blue flag with fifty stars fluttered in the wind as the colors of a glorious sunset filled the western sky. Caroline had seen this flag before. For but a moment, she tasted freedom, if only within the confines of a dream.

But this was more than a dream.

Caroline could smell the fragrance of nearby roses and hear the birds chirping in the trees. The cool evening breeze blowing against her cheek and through her hair could not be denied.

But there was something more.

Within her spirit, Caroline could sense God's pleasure. He was here in this place. He was with those who served under the flag of the thirteen stars. It was only by His grace that they would see victory, that fact was etched within her as if God had personally written it upon her heart.

As the sun dipped below the horizon, the flag of fifty stars slowly faded, but not the freedom it represented. That would remain embedded within Caroline's soul.

****

The December air grew colder as they marched toward Valley Forge. The gray, dismal sky seemed to echo what lived in the hearts of Washington's Army. A string of defeats lay behind them, and now a long winter stood before them. The war seemed endless, hopeless—futile.

But if only the others could see what Caroline had experienced. Perhaps, hope could be nourished and blossom into victory within them. But few seem to carry the faith to believe.

Nathan, however, wasn't one of them.

"So where do you think you were during your dream? Were there any recognizable landmarks?" Nathan asked after Caroline had shared with him the second dream of the flag from the future.

"I don't know where in the Colonies this was. The place within the dream was different than in the first one I had, though the flag looked the same."

"Fifty colonies." Nathan chuckled. "Still, hard to imagine that there will be that many."

Caroline glanced over. "I thought you believed me."

"Oh, I do. Wish you'd have a dream showing a map of the fifty colonies, though. I would love to know what that looks like. I suppose if we do win, they won't be colonies any longer. I believe I heard they'd be called states, instead."

"A flag of fifty stars." Franklin mocked as he walked nearby. "Sounds to me like that musket ball in Germantown hit you in the head harder than we thought. All this talk is nonsense."

"Maybe." Nathan shrugged. "But what if it's true? Wouldn't that give hope if we knew that we'd be victorious in—"

"It's false hope," Franklin growled. "I wouldn't be surprised if some of the generals have put her up to this to try and rally us. Well, I won't have any part of this. It's hogwash—"

"Then you might as well just go home," Caroline growled back at Franklin. "You're nothing more than a—"

"Easy." Nathan grabbed hold of Caroline's arm with a firm look on his face.

Caroline frowned and held her tongue from giving that man a further lashing. How could the dream of freedom come true with men like Franklin half-heartedly fighting the British?

****

— A PATRIOT'S DREAM —

The thin layer of snow crunched beneath Caroline's feet as she slowly marched ahead along with thousands of her comrades and their families. Some of the fire in Caroline's belly had mellowed after several days of retreating farther away from Philadelphia and the British troops. She felt more like a refugee without a home than a soldier fighting for freedom. There were many comforts of living in a house that she now longed for.

During the journey, Caroline passed many within this ragtag army who had tattered clothes and others who marched in worn-out boots with parts of their feet exposed. There was little hope of having these needs met anytime soon.

On the eighth day, they arrived at their destination some eighteen miles from Philadelphia.

Nestled between two large hills, Valley Forge was a small community built around ironworks and farming. The valley also housed some of the ammunition and supplies for the Continental Army, though Caroline was told much of it had been captured and destroyed by the British several months earlier.

"So, this is it?" Caroline glanced around at the snowy landscape with a sour look on her face.

"This is home." Nathan nodded. "Probably for the next several months."

Caroline took a deep breath, seeking to push away the hopelessness that tried to seep in. When she initially joined this fight in September, she imagined several battles, each of which would push the British closer to the sea until they finally surrendered. But she had been naive in her thinking. Any kind of victory now seemed years away.

"How are you holding up?" Caroline's father walked up beside her.

She shrugged. "Fine."

"This is the life of a soldier." He put his arm around her. "That's why I thought it best for you to go to North Carolina and stay with Aunt—"

"I can do this." Caroline set her jaw, determined not to back down.

He smiled. "I know you can."

— A PATRIOT'S DREAM —

— A PATRIOT'S DREAM —

Valley Forge
January 1778

"They who can give up essential liberty to obtain a little temporary safety deserve neither liberty nor safety."
Benjamin Franklin

Not long after they arrived at Valley Forge, the soldiers went to work building log barracks all along a section of the valley. These damp, cold structures were to be their homes indefinitely. It was better than staying in a tent during the winter but nothing like a cozy house with a fireplace.

Christmas Day came and went with little fanfare. Exchanging gifts and eating delicious holiday meals were things of the past. Now they simply struggled to survive, hoping to get some of the food rations promised by General Washington.

"So how did you celebrate Christmas when you were a child?" Nathan asked while he and Caroline collected firewood.

"Mama cooked a ham—sometimes a turkey. We'd have stuffing and yams with cinnamon." She stopped and reminisced as the sun began to set. "I can almost smell them now. God, I took all that for granted."

"We all did. Heck, I took something as simple as my warm bed for granted." He chuckled. "What I'd give for it now."

Caroline's thoughts returned to the present. "What do you think's going to happen? I know you've heard what many of the soldiers have said."

"Mutiny and desertion?" Nathan solemnly nodded. "Scarce provisions can bring out the worst in people. It's definitely possible."

"But—" Caroline's shoulders slumped. "If our army falls apart then the British win. But they *can't* win. They're *not supposed* to." She sighed as tears filled her eyes. "Maybe it was all just a stupid dream. I thought it was real, but everything seems to be crumbling away. We're losing the war and will never have a chance if the soldiers—"

"Caroline." Nathan set his bundle of wood down in the snow. "I made you a Christmas gift and think now's a good time to give it to you."

"You did?" Caroline dropped her wood and wiped the tears from her eyes.

"My mother taught me how to sew when I was younger. I've kept a few spools of thread in my pack along with a needle. After hearing your dream about the fifty stars, I had an idea."

"What idea?"

"Well, I tore my handkerchief in half and made a flag." Nathan pulled something out of his coat pocket. "It's not quite as blue and red as the colors of a real flag but close."

Caroline took the piece of material the size of her hand as fresh tears rose. "It's like the flag I saw."

Nathan nodded. "I made sure there were fifty white spots—stars. That was quite a challenge for something so small."

"I don't know what to say." Caroline studied the flag that Nathan had tediously worked on.

"Say that you'll never stop believing in your dream. When you feel like your hope's waning, pull this flag out and let it bring encouragement to you." He smiled. "I believe in your dream—in you. We *will* win this war."

"Thank you." Caroline hugged Nathan. "This means more to me than you know."

"You're welcome." His smile widened. "Now, let's say we get this wood back before the fire goes out, and our comrades become icicles."

Caroline laughed, thankful to have someone who believed in her and shared her burden of hope.

****

One night as Caroline slept, she found herself within a dream moving back and forth on a tree swing. She was at her childhood home just outside of New York City. The air was fresh and crisp, and a blue sky shone overhead as she kicked her legs, swinging as hard as she could.

"Looks like you've really gotten better at that," Caroline's mother said as she walked by with a basket of clean laundry to hang up in the warm sun.

"Yes, I can really go high." Caroline kicked her legs even harder, wanting to reach the top of the trees—the clouds in the sky. Maybe when she grew a little taller, she'd be able to do so.

Caroline glanced over as her mother set down the clothes basket. "I want to help!"

"You're not quite tall enough, sweetheart." Her mother pulled one of the garments out. "Won't be long, though."

"I can still help." Caroline dragged her feet on the ground to slow the momentum, then jumped out of the swing and stumbled before gaining her balance. She ran like a shot to the front porch, grabbed a wooden stool, and joined her mother.

"See." Caroline stepped up on the stool and grinned. "Now, I'm almost as tall as you."

Her mother smirked. "Not quite, but I suppose you're tall enough to help with the laundry."

Caroline took one of her father's shirts and two clothespins. "One day I'll be doing laundry all by myself."

The clumsily secured shirt she clipped slipped off the line and fell to the ground.

"Careful, Caroline." Her mother picked up the shirt and shook the dirt off. "Remember, if you're going to do this, you need to do it right or everything will have to be rewashed."

"I'm sorry, Mama."

"That's okay. Just take your time. This is not a race."

"I know." Caroline frowned. "I just wanted to do it as fast as you do."

"In time you will. For now, just learn how to do it correctly." Her mother paused. "It's like that with everything in life. If you don't learn the right way to do something, then quite often, you'll have to do it over again."

Caroline thought for a moment about her mother's wisdom. This was a good idea for most things, but not with schoolwork and chores. Those were things Caroline didn't like to do. The sooner she got done with them, the better, whether they were perfect or not.

"In everything you do, Caroline, seek to do your best at it," her mother added as if knowing Caroline's thoughts.

"Everything?" Caroline whined.

Her mother nodded. "My grandfather used to tell me that. It seemed like a bad idea when I was a child, but it made sense as I grew older."

"I suppose," Caroline mumbled as she clipped a pair of stockings to the clothesline.

"If you do your best at everything and do it right, I believe you can accomplish almost anything and have no regrets along the way."

Caroline relished this dream from a memory of long ago. That moment with her mother had greatly impacted Caroline, making her more determined than ever to excel at everything she did and not give up when faced with difficulties.

In fact, those difficulties only served as opportunities for Caroline to conquer and overcome them. Backing down from an obstacle was no longer in her blood.

She opened her eyes in the darkness of the barracks as the dream ended. For a moment, she just lay there in deep thought. What if she had not listened to her mother? Would Caroline be the same person she was now? Would she even have had the courage to fight as a soldier for her country? Probably not.

"Thank you, Mama," Caroline whispered to herself, wishing her mother could hear her. "I miss you so much."

In her mind's eye, she could see her mother's smile, and a strange peace filled Caroline's soul. One day, she'd see her mother again, and there'd be no war or death to come between them. For now, Caroline would take the life lessons she had learned and make the most of each day.

****

Weeks into the new year, the news of dead soldiers began to surface. But they didn't die in battle against the British but in the battle with sickness and starvation. Death even began to take some of the horses.

Supply wagons came here and there, but it was never enough. If the British were to attack, the Continental Army wouldn't have the strength or means with which to fight. Maybe coming to Valley Forge had been a mistake.

Despite it all, Caroline held on tightly to her dream of freedom, often pulling out the flag Nathan had sewn as a reminder.

"There's talk of them replacing Washington." A man spoke while a handful of soldiers warmed themselves around an outside fire in the early evening.

"Well, they best do something soon or there won't be enough of us to fight with," a blond-headed soldier added. "If we want to win this—"

"Be realistic!" Franklin cut in. "We must all be realistic. Do we really think we can beat the British? They have training, food, and supplies. All we have is this." He lifted his worn boot with a stocking showing through it.

Franklin made Caroline's blood boil. "Then why are you fighting?" she blurted out. "Why even bother if you don't believe we can win?"

It was quite clear from Franklin's expression that he still had no great love for Caroline either. "Because, little missy, we may not be able to win the war, but we can cause the British enough grief that they'll ease the hardship upon us. That's really all we want."

"If the king would agree to some of our concessions, I'd be willing to lay down my arms and end this war." Another soldier nodded.

"What concessions did you have in mind?" the blond-headed soldier asked.

Slowly, several of Caroline's comrades began listing what they'd be willing to accept from Great Britain in exchange for an end to the war.

"And what happens if the king agrees to these concessions, and you hand over your arms to him." Nathan stepped into the conversation. "What's to prevent the king from changing his mind?"

"We'd hold him accountable or start the war back up," Franklin replied snidely.

"With what?" Nathan shrugged. "The king would undoubtedly take away your ability to challenge the empire ever again. Our condition would be worse than it was to begin with."

"What do you know, boy?" Franklin frowned. "Compromise is our best bet at seeing—"

"No, no, no!" Caroline yelled. "We will never be *free* if we compromise! Can't you see that? God has made a way for us to be free. All we have to do is not give up."

"You have a silly, stupid dream, and now you're a military expert and politician. Perhaps you should be General Washington's advisor." Franklin mocked. His eyes then narrowed on Caroline. "Why don't you go home, little girl? You *don't* belong here. This is no place for children who—"

"Because she believes in freedom, and you, sir, believe in giving all that up for a warm meal and a cozy bed." Nathan's voice rose. "I dare say that she's twice the soldier you are."

Franklin shot up from his seat and pointed his finger at Nathan. "You best recant that, boy, or I'll put you in your place."

Nathan slowly stood with an unyielding expression. "I speak only the truth, and for that, I *will not* recant."

"Why you sorry little—" Franklin lunged toward Nathan with his fist rearing back.

Nathan dodged the blow and cut Franklin's legs out from beneath him, sending the man hard to the ground. Rage shot across Franklin's face as he stood back up and snatched a solid limb from the stack of firewood.

"I'm going to kill you, boy, and save the British the trouble." Franklin swung but missed Nathan.

After he swung and missed again, Nathan lowered his shoulder and rammed into Franklin, sending them both to the ground. Each managed to get in a blow before Franklin pushed Nathan over and tried to pin him down.

Caroline jumped on Franklin's back. "Get off him!" she yelled and began pounding on his head.

"What's going on here?" a voice called out from behind them.

As Caroline and the men glanced over toward the voice, they froze. General Washington and his aid stood behind them with firm expressions on their faces. Caroline slid off Franklin's back while Franklin released his grip on Nathan.

Nathan wiped his bloody lip and quickly stood tall, straightening up his coat. "Just a bit of a disagreement, sir. It won't happen again."

Caroline, too, stood up straight. She had seen the general from a distance before but never up close. This, however, was not an occasion that she wished to be graced by his presence.

"As you were." The general stepped closer and sat down on a tree stump beside the soldiers. The fire reflected off his face as he looked each of them in the eye. "I know our situation is dire, but I implore you not to lose heart. If we turn on one another then we've already lost. The enemy would like nothing better for that to happen. But it can't. Do I make myself clear?"

"Yes, sir," a few of the men responded in unison.

Caroline studied the general, wondering if his intentions of freedom were still set in stone or if those intentions had been compromised as they had with Franklin. Was General Washington truly the leader they needed or was there someone else?

"We are in this war to win it, aren't we, sir?" Caroline blurted out. "No compromises, right—sir?"

A faint groan came from Nathan as if he was displeased or, perhaps, in disbelief that Caroline had asked such an audacious question.

General Washington's expression eased into a faint smile. "What's your name, soldier?"

"Caroline, sir," she responded, wondering if maybe she should have kept her mouth shut.

"Caroline?" The general's eyes widened as if surprised to see a female soldier among the men.

"Yes, sir. Caroline Johnson."

"Caroline Johnson." The general pursed his lips together. "Yes, I do remember that name coming up in conversation with General Sullivan a few months ago." Washington's expression firmed as he looked into her eyes. "There is only one outcome of this war we will accept, and that is victory. Without it, we will never be free."

Franklin's gaze trailed off to the ground. Any thought of compromise would not be addressed now.

"Thank you, sir," Caroline responded with a faint smile of her own.

"Gentlemen—and lady." General Washington gave a nod to Caroline. "Our stance in this war must be clear." He glanced around at each of the soldiers. "As once said by my friend and colleague, Patrick Henry, 'Give me liberty or give me death.' That should be our battle cry. Nothing less will suffice. If we stay true to our convictions, I believe, with the help of our Lord, we will be victorious."

Caroline's heart warmed. Despite the string of defeats they had faced under General Washington's command, and the complaints reeled against his leadership, he was the right man to lead this army. Caroline was sure of it. She would remain loyal to his calling as long as she fought under his command.

****

The months at Valley Forge seemed to be full of blessings and curses. In January, the French declared war on the British and began to aid the Americans. Now, King George would have to be concerned with more than just the Colonies. Every territory the British ruled might be challenged by the French. The British military would be spread thin. This was a major blessing.

— A PATRIOT'S DREAM —

In February, Von Steuben, a military officer from the Prussian Army arrived at Valley Forge as the new Inspector General. Though he couldn't speak or write English, his plan was to teach the Continental Army new ways to combat the British.

"One of the problems that the Inspector General has noticed is our technique." An officer in Caroline's regiment stood before the troops with a copy of a notice from Von Steuben.

Caroline and Nathan exchanged glances, wondering where this was going.

The officer continued. "Currently, soldiers from each colony have their own way of doing drills and maneuvers. For the army to be unified and work efficiently together, there will be one method used for the entire Continental Army from now on. Today begins the first lesson."

Nathan leaned closer to Caroline. "Guess we'll see if one can truly teach an old dog new tricks," he whispered.

Though Caroline was new to the army, many of the men around her had been fighting since the war began. She wondered how well they would take to learning a new way of fighting. The disgruntled expressions on some of their faces revealed their displeasure.

"This will be interesting," she whispered back to Nathan.

Each day, they learned new techniques, drills, and maneuvers, most of which were quite different than what they had been doing. No longer would they form a long column when going into battle as the British did. They would march in smaller, compact formations. The former Prussian commander also sought to get the soldiers in better physical shape.

At first, Caroline wasn't so sure about this man, but as the days of winter moved on, she could begin to see the fruits of his labor.

Not only had her regiment become better organized on the parade ground but they had increased in marching speed and were more effective in combat maneuvers.

But mingled in with these blessings was a curse of death throughout the camp. Hundreds of soldiers were dying of sickness and disease even as Spring neared. Now Caroline's father was sick with what the doctor suspected to be pneumonia.

"How were things today?" her father asked when Caroline came into the barracks.

"Tiring. We practiced a lot. Next week we're going to officially celebrate our alliance with France. Von Steuben expects us to be in top form when we line up for inspection. How are you feeling?"

"I'm holding my own, I suppose."

She sat on the edge of the bed and put her hand on his forehead. "Papa, you feel hotter today."

He nodded as he took short shallow breaths. Caroline felt helpless. Each day, he seemed to be getting worse, not better as she had been fervently praying for. Her father had to get well. He was all she had left.

"You've become a beautiful young woman." He reached up and touched her cheek as she put a cool compress on his forehead. "Your mother would be so proud."

"Thank you, Papa."

"I know Nathan has taken notice of you."

Caroline could feel herself blush, though what her father said was no lie. Over the months since she met Nathan, he had become her best friend. But feelings within her heart began to stir for him lately, feelings she had never known before. From the look in Nathan's eyes at times, he must be experiencing the same.

Her father had said little until now, though he wasn't blind to it.

"I think Nathan is a fine young man." A faint smile rose on her father's pale face.

"Papa." Caroline grinned bashfully.

"He will love and protect you." His father wheezed.

"Papa, why are you saying this."

"Nathan spoke to me a few days ago." Her father took hold of Caroline's hand. "I gave him my blessing."

Caroline was taken aback. She was fifteen and Nathan, seventeen. That was not much younger than when her parents married. Still, was now the time for marriage? Death loomed all around while their enemy sat fewer than twenty miles to the east. Caroline's main focus had been freedom. Not love.

"I—I don't think I'm ready, Papa," Caroline blurted out.

"That's okay." Her father squeezed her hand. "You'll know when the time is right."

She nodded. The idea of romance seemed so out of place right now. Maybe later in the future. Marriage and raising a family while under the oppression of the British Empire and the uncertainty of war would be challenging. She desired the covenant of marriage to be born within freedom.

"I also want to apologize to you, Caroline."

"Apologize?" Her eyes narrowed. "Why?"

"You are passionate about the dream of freedom. I thought maybe it was just a dream at first and discouraged you from believing in it." He sighed. "I was wrong to do so. Caroline, I can see that this was more than just a dream. You passionately share this conviction with others with the hope that it will encourage them. Forgive me for trying to douse the fire of that which is dear to you."

"Oh, Papa." Caroline smiled. "There's nothing to forgive."

"I would never want to hurt you in any way." His eyes welled up. "I love you, Caroline, and want to encourage you to continue pursuing *the dream*."

"I will, Papa." She leaned down and hugged him, thankful to have his blessing and confidence. "Now, let's work on getting you better."

Three days later, however, her father lost his battle with pneumonia and died during the night in his sleep. His death was a crushing blow to Caroline. She had lost everything that was precious to her. The war had seen to that.

— **A PATRIOT'S DREAM** —

― A PATRIOT'S DREAM ―

June 1778
New Jersey

"I tremble for my country when I reflect that God is just; that his justice cannot sleep forever."
Thomas Jefferson

Spring gave way to Summer and an end to the encampment at Valley Forge. The months there had been like a bitter herb, mixed in with elements of sweetness. In the end, Caroline was glad to leave the pain and sorrow of the valley, though she found it a struggle to set her gaze on the future.

Caroline and Nathan marched quickly in the hot, muggy weather along with the troops under the command of Major General Charles Lee. With the French inclusion into the war, the British had their hands full. Apparently, feeling they were spread too thin, the Redcoats evacuated Philadelphia and headed to New York.

Despite the British relinquishing the American capital, General Washington didn't want to let them leave without a fight. Over the last couple of days, Caroline's regiment had shadowed the British troops, seeking to find a weak point and exploit it.

"You've been quiet. How are you doing?" Nathan whispered as they marched.

She shrugged. "Fine."

The truth was, Caroline wasn't fine. She hadn't been herself over the last few months. When her father passed away, a part of her died with him. Now, she felt all alone in her war-torn country with the only light being Nathan.

"This may have been a good fight for you to sit out of until you're feeling—"

"I'm fine!" Caroline snapped. She closed her eyes and sighed. "I'm sorry."

Nathan managed a smile. "No apologies needed. Just stay focused on the task at hand today. I don't want to have to worry about you."

"You don't have to worry about me." She frowned. "I'm not a little girl who's never fought in—"

"I didn't say you were, but being out of sorts can make it hard to focus on—"

"I'm fine!" she growled.

"Very well then." Nathan kept his gaze ahead.

— A PATRIOT'S DREAM —

She berated herself for being ugly to Nathan. He didn't deserve that. Nathan was a patient man, always slow to anger and quick to encourage.

Caroline's father had been right about him. Three weeks ago, Nathan asked for her hand in marriage, and she accepted with one stipulation. They would wait until the war was over before they entered into the binding covenant of love.

Despite the excitement over the engagement with Nathan, the pain of losing her entire family weighed heavily upon Caroline. It was a heaviness she couldn't seem to shake off.

As they approached Monmouth, New Jersey, their regiment stopped and waited. The British Army appeared to be split into two sections. It became clear that Major General Lee's plan was to engage the rear of the British Army and inflict as much damage as they could.

All their training over the winter months under Von Steuben would soon be tested. Despite feeling out of sorts, Caroline hoped for victory. If they all could just keep their wits about themselves, maybe it would happen.

In the heat of the day, Major General Lee gave the order for the Americans to move into the township. The surprise attack began.

Caroline wiped the sweat from her brow, took aim, and fired. Though it had been over six months since their last battle, she hadn't lost her edge with the rifle. A British soldier fell to the ground.

"That's for Papa." She quickly grabbed another musket pack from her bag and reloaded her rifle.

The Americans had the element of surprise and pressed ahead. Not long into the battle, however, the main force of the British Army appeared, flooding into the township. As fighting grew heavier, some of the American militia who had joined them began to withdraw from the battle.

"Hey—where are you going?" Nathan yelled at the retreating men. "Come back!"

What looked promising at first quickly turned sour like in previous battles. Fear rose up, giving way to panic and chaos. Something had to change, or they'd never win the war.

Nathan fired his rifle and looked over at Caroline. "I want you to fall back. It's getting too dangerous."

She ignored his request and quickly squatted down behind a tree trunk to reload. This was probably no more dangerous than the last two battles they had fought in. The only difference was that Nathan had more to lose now because of their growing relationship.

"Caroline! Did you hear me? I want you—"

"I don't care what you want! I'm not leaving!" While still crouched down, Caroline swung her rifle over the tree trunk, pointed it at the approaching Redcoats, and pulled the trigger.

Nathan muttered something under his breath as he took aim at their enemy. Caroline had sometimes been called hardheaded by her father and strong-willed by her mother. Nathan would just have to learn to accept her as she was.

She glanced over at him while reloading. Perhaps the wedding engagement had been a mistake. A war was certainly not the time for them to grow closer to one another. In fact, maybe the friendship, itself, was a bad idea. The emptiness within her heart grew as the battle raged on.

Caroline put her gaze back on the enemy, deciding to fight to the end whether in victory or defeat. The pain of losing her family had stolen the joy that she once held for life. If death came today. . . so be it.

The sound of a cannon blast thundered, and an explosion some fifty feet away shook the ground.

"Fall back, Caroline!" Nathan yelled as he scampered backward.

"You go on! I'm staying!"

"We're going to be overrun, Caroline!"

Caroline clasped her jaw, regretting the day she had ever met this man.

Another cannon ball exploded only closer this time. The enemy continued moving in on the American's position. If Caroline waited much longer, she would get cut off with no means of escape. A musket ball scalped the top of the tree trunk she hid behind, just missing her head. Her heart raced. Should she stay and die or run and save her skin? Caroline felt frozen in place.

Just then, an explosion hit nearby, its force knocking Caroline over.

"Come on!" Nathan yanked Caroline up by the arm.

The two scampered away along with a handful of other soldiers as the British quickly moved in. Caroline fully expected to get shot in the back, though that never happened.

Their run for safety came to an abrupt halt outside the township. General Washington had just arrived with the bulk of the Continental Army.

Caroline leaned over, catching her breath as sweat poured down her face. If only battles could happen in the warm spring, not in the frigid winter or in the heat of summer.

Washington quickly reorganized his troops and counterattacked the British. The battle raged on into the early evening. Caroline felt utterly exhausted by the time the Redcoats fell back to a position on the other side of the township.

When dawn came, the British had disappeared, slipping away under the cover of darkness as they continued their retreat to New York. Though not a victory, the battle was not a defeat either. The Americans held their ground, not giving way to the Redcoats. Maybe that was something to build upon.

Later that day, Caroline sat beside a tree, cleaning her rifle. She and Nathan had talked little since the fight with the British. It was better that way. There was still a part of Caroline that wished that the battle had claimed her life, ending the heaviness that draped around her.

Nathan walked over with his rifle in hand. "May I join you?"

Caroline said nothing, keeping her gaze on the task at hand.

"May I join you, Caroline?" He repeated the question only a little louder this time.

She nodded without looking up.

Nathan sat down and began cleaning his own rifle. "Are you angry with me?"

Angry? No, she just hated him or, at least, wanted to. If only she could loathe Nathan. That would make it so much easier to distance herself from him.

"I said, are you—"

"No!" Caroline replied sharply.

"Well, you're doing a good job of pretending to be, I suppose," he said light-heartedly.

Caroline sighed and shook her head, though she kept her focus on the rifle as she began cleaning it for a second time. Maybe Nathan would get bored and leave if she kept silent.

Nathan stopped what he was doing. "Look, Caroline, I'm not your enemy."

"I never said you were." She spoke through clenched teeth.

"Maybe not, but your actions speak louder than your words."

"I don't like you telling me what to do!" she yelled.

Nathan's eyes widened. "I don't recall ordering you around—"

"Look!" She stopped and stared at him with a scowl on her face. "I feel like you're always watching over me, making sure I get enough to eat or making sure no one dishonors me. You order me around in battle—"

"You're very important to me, Caroline. I want to make sure you're taken care of, and I want to protect you—"

"I don't need your protection or your help or anything else for that matter!"

Nathan looked at her incredulously. "I love you, Caroline. Love protects and cares for those under its wing. I'm not trying to control or order you around. I simply love you and want—"

"Then just stop—loving me," Caroline blurted out.

"What?" Nathan's brows tightened. "I—I don't understand. I thought we cared for one another."

The words pricked Caroline's heart which she had tried to harden toward him. She did love him, more than anyone else. But that love scared her. Why did it scare her? Why was she pushing him away? As emotions churned, the tears came, though she tried to banish them.

"Caroline?" Nathan's voice softened. "Do you love me?"

"Yes—but I'm afraid," she sobbed. "Each time I lose someone that I love, the pain is just so—" She shook her head. "I—I can't lose you too."

Caroline lowered her head and began weeping, feeling distraught and hopeless. Why had she allowed herself to have feelings for this man? It would only lead to pain.

Nathan crawled over and sat beside Caroline, pulling her close as she cried. He said nothing because he could promise nothing other than his love for her. Life was dark and filled with uncertainty. There were no guarantees of another sunrise, much less a life of happiness together.

"For as long as I have breath, Caroline, I promise to love you and you alone." He kissed her on the head and squeezed her tightly.

That was all Caroline could ask for. All she could give. "And I promise the same to you."

As the tears slowed, the burden she had carried eased as if a divine hand had lifted it from her shoulders. Love without the certainty of tomorrow was a risk. But without love, she had nothing. The risk was worth the possibility of pain. It had to be.

— A PATRIOT'S DREAM —

— A PATRIOT'S DREAM —

Rhode Island
August 1778

"I always consider the settlement of America with reverence and wonder, as the opening of a grand scene and design in providence, for the illumination of the ignorant and the emancipation of the slavish part of mankind all over the earth."
John Adams

The hot summer continued, but that didn't stop the fighting. Under General Sullivan's command, Caroline and Nathan marched with their comrades toward Newport to engage the British. This time the French would be joining them in battle and improve the odds of victory.

The misty, gray skies had brought cooler temperatures over the last few days, a welcome reprieve from the heat.

"Looks like the storm is moving farther away from shore." Nathan eyed the eastern horizon.

"I'm glad it didn't come inland." Caroline looked up into the partly cloudy moonlit sky. "Drizzle's one thing but fighting in pouring rain is another."

"Most definitely."

Caroline shifted the rifle on her shoulder. "How many of the French do you think will be joining us in the fight?"

"Not sure. A few thousand, possibly."

The French had docked their ships days earlier with plans to land their troops. But when the British fleet was spotted closing in, the French ships left to engage them. Then the skies off the coast became dark as a great storm raged out in the sea.

Now, General Sullivan's Army moved on Newport to seize the city and cut the British off from reinforcements. The plan, however, was contingent on the French landing their troops.

Caroline glanced down at her left hand where a small silver ring sat on her third finger. Last month, Nathan made the marriage engagement complete with the ring. It had been his mother's wedding band before her passing. She had promised it to Nathan who had been her only child.

Nathan briefly slid his hand into Caroline's and squeezed it. "I love you," he whispered.

A smile rose on Caroline's face. "And I love you."

He removed his hand, not wanting to draw too much attention to them. If only the war could end tomorrow, and they could marry and move back to Philadelphia or perhaps to the countryside. Caroline was tempted to dream of what that might look like but now was not the time. Their complete focus needed to be on the moment as they prepared to fight the British.

The following day, the atmosphere of confidence within the army had been thrown into disarray.

"What did you find out?" Caroline asked as Nathan approached.

"The rumors are true." He stopped in front of her. "The French aren't coming. Their fleet is heading to Boston instead. Something about damaged ships from the storm."

"Well, that's just lovely." Caroline sighed loudly in disappointment.

"I've heard that General Sullivan's hotter than a boiling steam kettle." Nathan removed his rifle from his shoulder. "I'm sure he'd like to give the French a piece of his mind."

"This changes everything, doesn't it?"

Nathan nodded. "I've also heard murmuring that some of the militia might not join us in battle now that the odds have changed in the Brit's favor."

"What?" Caroline's brows furrowed.

Frustration rose within her as, yet another possible victory seemed to be unraveling.

A few days later, under the cover of darkness, General Sullivan gave the order for his troops to withdraw. With the loss of the American militia units and the abandonment by the French army, Sullivan's depleted forces would be unable to maintain the siege of Newport, especially with word that British reinforcements would be arriving.

So, without as much as a shot being fired, Caroline retreated with her comrades.

She and Nathan marched near the rear of the formation. Caroline fought discouragement. The war seemed like it would never end. For each step forward, it felt like they would take an equal step backward—sometimes two steps backward. Victory was elusive. But it would come. It had to. The dreams God had given her were proof of it, weren't they?

"I know that look." Nathan glanced over as they retreated northward. "Things are not as bad as they seem."

She nodded. Nathan knew her well. As the months went by, the fire of freedom that had once burned brightly within Caroline's soul began to flicker. Nathan, however, had been a constant source of encouragement, often fanning the flame of hope back to life.

"We'll regroup and try again," Nathan continued. "The British are going to have their hands full battling us and the French in the future. I believe at some point, they'll realize this isn't worth it and eventually give up."

Caroline looked over and managed a smile. "Thank you."

"For what?" Nathan's right brow rose.

"You always have a way of looking at the brighter side of bad situations. I really need to hear it sometimes." Caroline glanced up into the sky as dawn approached. "You remind me of my father in some ways."

"Well, I consider that an honor. He was a good man."

"What is your father like?" Caroline asked.

"He's kind of like me, I suppose, but doesn't always see the good in every situation. When Mama died, he seemed to become a little harder around the edges. Can't blame him." Nathan sighed. "When he sent me Mama's wedding ring, he didn't include a letter or even a brief note to let me know how he was doing."

"Do you think he's still angry with you for leaving to fight in the war?"

Nathan shrugged. "I don't know. There were others who could help him with his business. I couldn't stay working in textiles while the British destroyed our country. I couldn't live with myself if I did."

"Maybe one day he'll understand."

"I can only hope that he—"

"Hold up." An officer called out. "We have reports that the British are going to try and cut us down from behind." He pointed to a section of a long stone wall they had just passed by. "Position yourself behind the there and wait for my instruction."

"Well, Caroline, it looks like we will fight after all." Nathan nearly smirked as they quickly moved into position behind a section of the wall.

"This isn't exactly how I had pictured the battle going, though." Caroline shook her head. "Now, the British have the upper hand—"

"Silence!" The officer quickly crouched down behind the wall with the rest of the contingent.

Within the quietness of early dawn, footsteps could be heard coming in their direction.

Caroline peered over the wall. "Redcoats." She quickly ducked down and whispered in Nathan's ear. "We're definitely outnumbered."

Nathan sighed quietly and pulled back the hammer on his rifle. Caroline followed suit. The footsteps grew louder as their enemy approached.

Her heart raced while emotions flooded her soul. Anything could happen in this battle. Nathan could die or they both could. Caroline cursed the fear. Now was not the time to entertain losing those she loved. Her focus must be on taking down the enemy.

"Fire!" Their officer yelled.

Caroline and her comrades slid their rifles over the wall and fired. Spent black powder from the American's muskets shot up in the air while several British soldiers fell to the ground. Caroline and Nathan ducked back down as the Redcoats returned fire, their shots ricocheting off the top of the stone wall.

"Those aren't just Redcoats. There's at least one Hessian regiment." Caroline quickly reloaded her rifle with a scowl on her face. "Blasted German mercenaries! I hate them almost as much as the British."

With the battle growing in intensity, the protection of the wall was no longer a viable option. They were outnumbered and would soon be overrun. Caroline's regiment pulled back and quickly retreated toward Turkey Hill.

Caroline wiped the sweat from her forehead in the heat of the late morning as the battle raged on. She had just been replenished with more musket packs which she slid into her pouch. The sound of gunshots and cannon blasts echoed from across the island as the enemy engaged more of the American forces.

Despite having the high ground, Redcoats and Hessians were too many, and quickly stormed the hill.

"Fall back!" The officer over Caroline's regiment yelled. "Fall back!"

Caroline and Nathan backpedaled while shooting, then turned and ran for the nearest cover with their comrades. She wondered what this battle might have looked like if the French had come as they promised. Would the Americans have retaken Rhode Island, lessening the British footprint in the colonies? They would never know.

Nathan shot his rifle and then ran, slipping in behind a tree where Caroline stood. "This is a bit tricky."

She nodded while catching her breath and reloading. The sun was growing hotter and the battle not going the way she had envisioned.

Part of General Nathan Greene's army was spread out just down from them. That's where Caroline's regiment would go to regroup.

After she fired her rifle, Caroline ran, heading toward the cover of another nearby tree. However, before she made it, Caroline stepped into a small hole and fell forward. She screamed in pain as she slammed against the ground.

"Oh, God, this hurts," Caroline grunted while struggling to her feet.

Her swift gate turned into a hobble as pain pulsated up through her ankle into her leg. This couldn't be happening.

— A PATRIOT'S DREAM —

While Caroline was out in the open, a musket ball whizzed right by her ear, sending a shiver of fear down her spine.

"Protect me, Lord," she whimpered with each step.

"Caroline, get down!" Nathan yelled while running toward her.

She dove to the ground, angry with herself while feeling hopeless at the same time. There was no way she could outrun the approaching enemy.

"Are you hit?" Nathan knelt beside her.

"No, I turned my stupid ankle." She grimaced as her eyes welled up. "I'm sorry. Go on without me—"

"Hold on." Nathan swung his rifle over his shoulder and picked her up into his arms. "I've got you."

Caroline started to object, not wanting Nathan to be harmed on her account but knew she would be wasting her breath.

Nathan broke into a slow jog as the retreat continued. Caroline felt helpless, more like a burden than a warrior. But God willing, they would live to see another day.

As they neared a section of General Greene's army, a cannonball fired from the approaching British exploded just to their right, nearly knocking Nathan down. He quickly regained his balance and continued ahead.

After passing through the general's troops, Nathan's pace slowed. When they were finally out of harm's way, he gently put her down and collapsed to the ground as he struggled to catch his breath.

Just then, British warships off the coast opened fire, launching explosive artillery toward American forces.

Caroline's eyes widened. "Maybe we should keep going."

"I think we're. . . out of reach." Nathan heaved in air. "We should be fine."

"I'm sorry." Caroline shook her head in disgust. "I shouldn't have been so clumsy."

"Not clumsy. . . fortunate. I'd rather twist an ankle. . . than get shot in the head." Nathan took a deep breath.

"I guess you're right. Thank you for—" Caroline's eyes narrowed on his right arm. "Nathan, you're bleeding."

He glanced down and placed his hand over his bloody arm. "I thought I felt a sting. Didn't know I'd been shot."

Caroline crawled over. "Take your coat off and let me check it."

"I'm sure it's just a little flesh wound." He slid off his coat. "Looks like now we've both gotten shot in battle. Maybe that will be our fill for this war."

"I hope so." Caroline rolled up his shirt sleeve and examined the wound. "Thank God, it just grazed you."

By afternoon, the battle with the British came to an end, despite their ships' continual artillery shelling toward the American defensive positions on the hilltops. Though the battle had not been victorious, it had not been a defeat either, although it felt that way to Caroline.

She limped over to the base of a tree and sat down, hating the feeling of helplessness that the injury brought. A moment later, Nathan joined her.

"Here's some stew." He handed her a bowl.

"Thank you, but you don't have to do that. I can get my own."

"That you could, but it will take longer for your ankle to heal if you keep walking on it. I know you don't want that."

"No, I don't." Caroline frowned, looking down at her ankle that was wrapped tight in cloth. "But I hate this."

"You'll be out of commission for a bit." Nathan put his arm around her. "Can't have you hobbling around like a lame duck while those Redcoats take potshots at you."

"Certainly, not." Caroline took a bite of the stew before shoveling it into her mouth, realizing she was hungrier than she thought.

When she was done, she leaned her head on Nathan's shoulder while he finished his meal. Caroline closed her eyes, feeling exhausted after getting little sleep over the last day. Despite the sound of British artillery blasts from their ships, she fell asleep.

As she slept, she found herself hiking uphill in a forest. Caroline stopped and looked around, wondering how she had gotten there. The sound of chirping birds and the smell of pine made it seem so real, though, within her spirit, she knew this must be a dream.

"The view is quite lovely at the top." A familiar voice spoke.

Caroline spun around. Her father stood beside her wearing a faint smile on his face and a sparkle in his eyes.

"Papa!" She wrapped her arms around him and buried her head in his chest. "I've missed you so much."

He squeezed Caroline and kissed her on the top of the head. "And I've missed you, little one."

She pulled back and looked up into his eyes. "I wish this wasn't just a dream."

"One day, that will be so." He gently caressed her cheek. "For now, I have something to show you."

The two continued hiking higher up a trail through the forest of evergreen.

Caroline's life on the battlefield and the wary months of surviving one oppressive day to another felt like a dream from a lifetime ago. Within this moment, the air was crisp, and the scenery was peaceful.

"Life can seem like a battle, Caroline." Her father spoke as they walked. "Sometimes, the biggest battle takes place up here." He tapped his head. "Within our heart, passion, faith, and life can abound. But within our mind, doubt, hopelessness, and fear can loom, making it difficult to live out what's in our heart."

Caroline nodded. "It really has been hard at times. I honestly just figured we'd be closer to victory and freedom by now. Some days, it feels like it may never come."

"Yes, gauging freedom from one battle to the next can breed hopelessness. But true freedom lives in here." He put his hand over his heart. "It's a freedom given from God and can never be enslaved or stolen. Guard your heart, little one, and you will always be free."

She hadn't thought about that before. Freedom truly came from the heart. The dreams of the flag of fifty stars had been sewn into her heart and had once been a burning fire of hope. The doubts and fear flowing from her mind had been dousing that flame.

"I'll try harder, Papa."

"Perhaps, this will help," he said as they stepped out of the forest into a clearing at the top of the mountain.

"Wow!" Caroline gasped. "It's so beautiful!"

Below her, a turquoise river flowed through a valley between blue and purple mountains capped in white. They seemed to go on as far as the eye could see. Caroline had never been on a mountaintop before, though she had hoped to do so one day.

"Is this the northwest territory on the western part of The Colonies?" she asked while panning around.

"No, little one. This is far away from the Thirteen Colonies." He put his arm over her shoulder. "One day this will be the forty-second star you've seen on the flag of fifty."

A chill ran down Caroline's spine followed by a wave of joy. This heavenly view had been afforded to her, one that few, if any, of her generation would ever see.

"This is part of what you now fight for, Caroline. Remember this moment when in the heat of battle, or on frostbitten days of winter. On those hopeless, lonely nights as you gaze up into the heavens, remember that God is for us —for freedom."

"I will, Papa." Caroline closed her eyes and breathed in deeply of the clean, crisp air, wishing not to leave this place but to remain in the future of freedom.

— A PATRIOT'S DREAM —

As her father kissed her on the head, a warmth washed over her, and the dream slowly faded.

****

The following day, Caroline gazed out from their hillside position into the inlet below. The British ships had ceased their barrage of artillery against the Americans. Caroline kept her weight on a makeshift crutch Nathan had made for her. For the next several weeks, she would be limited to staying at their encampment while her ankle slowly healed.

"Beautiful view, isn't it." Nathan walked up behind her.

"I suppose. If not for the British warships, it might be prettier."

"True." He put his arm around her. "How's your ankle?"

"It feels about the same. That stupid hole," she muttered. "I can't believe this happened."

A compassionate smile rose on Nathan's face. "I'm sorry. Grateful nothing worse happened, though."

"I know." Caroline sighed. "But I want to be able to pull my load, not sit around, waiting for this stupid thing to heal."

"When I was a boy and things seemed to go awry, my mother would remind me that God causes all things to work for the good of His people. I wasn't sure how that applied to everything in my life, but it got me thinking a little differently about the difficulties we face. Maybe there's a reason for this injury."

"Like what?"

"Well—" Nathan paused as he thought. "Maybe it will be good for you to accept help from others. You can be quite hardheaded at times and try to do everything on your own." A smile rose on his face. "This injury will force you to receive people's help whether you want to or not."

Caroline rolled her eyes, though, in her heart, she knew Nathan was right. She wanted to be self-sufficient. Maybe it was because Caroline was a woman in a man's army, and she wanted to prove her worth. Or maybe it was because she was the only one left in her family to carry on the fight.

"I guess so." Caroline shrugged. "Still, I wish it hadn't happened."

Nathan chuckled. "That makes two of us."

When Caroline turned around, she noticed the soldiers were beginning to take down the encampment. "What's going on?"

"I don't know. Let's find out."

"Are we leaving?" Nathan asked as he and Caroline approached some of their comrades.

One of the soldiers nodded. "News has it that several thousand Redcoats are preparing to land in Newport. We'll no longer be able to hold our position in a fight. General Washington has ordered an immediate evacuation. He wants us out of here by nightfall before the British arrive."

"Well, so much for taking back Rhode Island." Caroline threw up her arms in disappointment.

"We live to fight another day," their comrade said before starting back with the dismantling of the encampment.

"That seems to be our motto," Caroline muttered to herself as she fought to be optimistic.

By early evening, she and Nathan boarded one of the ships that carried them across the channel to Bristol.

Caroline pulled out the small flag of fifty stars that Nathan had made for her and rubbed her fingers over the surface of it. She then glanced back at the island and sighed.

One day, it would be free of British control along with the rest of The Colonies. If only that day could come sooner than later.

— A PATRIOT'S DREAM —

— A PATRIOT'S DREAM —

October 1778

"The spirit of resistance to government is so valuable on certain occasions that I wish it to be always kept alive."
Thomas Jefferson

Caroline stood beside Nathan wearing their tattered uniforms as they both faced the pastor of a countryside church. She glanced up at Nathan and smiled. He was her best friend and though young, was a man of proven character—a man she desired to spend the rest of her life with.

As the British forces turned their attention to attacking the Southern colonies, it became clear the war would not be ending any time soon. Freedom from British tyranny may be years away. If Caroline and Nathan were going to be fighting side by side, there was no longer a good reason not to do so together as one within God's eyes.

"I now pronounce you husband and wife." The pastor finished the brief ceremony and smiled. "You may kiss the bride, Nathan."

Caroline's heartbeat quickened as she looked into Nathan's eyes. They had never kissed before. In fact, Caroline had never romantically kissed a man before.

Nathan smiled and leaned in, pressing his lips to hers. The kiss was warm, tender, and inviting. Within the simple kiss, Caroline felt closer to Nathan as if a wall had been broken down, allowing for greater intimacy. Her best friend was now her husband.

After the ceremony, the two stepped out of the church and walked beside a creek, arm in arm under the red and yellow trees of autumn. The moment felt surreal and strange yet delightful.

"I wish my family could have been here." Caroline leaned her head against his shoulder after they sat down next to the creek.

"I wish the same." Nathan put his arm around her. "I know your family and my mother are smiling down from Heaven."

Silence followed as the two sat there. Caroline's thoughts shifted from the past to the future. With marriage now behind them, she was free to dream, if only a little, about what life with Nathan would be like. How many children would they have? Where would they live when the war came to an end?

Over a year ago when she was fourteen, these questions would have never been on the forefront of Caroline's mind.

Now, she had just turned sixteen, maturing in the fire of affliction and seeing life from a totally different perspective.

"I love you." Nathan kissed her.

She kissed him back. This binding love would be tested each day as they faced life in the midst of a raging war.

When she looked into Nathan's eyes, uncertainty rose, and fear of losing her beloved in battle washed over Caroline. The pain instantly became unbearable, seeking to crush her.

As if knowing her thoughts, Nathan gently stroked her cheek. "That's not worth thinking about, Caroline. Our lives are in the Almighty's hands. That's where we have to leave them and continue this fight together."

Caroline nodded as she struggled to release the thoughts. Though she and Nathan were now married, their focus would still be on the task at hand. *Freedom.*

— A PATRIOT'S DREAM —

— A PATRIOT'S DREAM —

New York
July 1779

"The spirit of resistance to government is so valuable on certain occasions that I wish it to be always kept alive."
Thomas Jefferson

    The year had been slow with little action as most of the fighting took place in the Southern Colonies. Small skirmishes had occurred around New York but nothing more than stalemates.

    A month earlier, General Sullivan had been dispatched by George Washington to battle the Loyalists and the majority the Iroquois Nation who had aligned themselves with the British. This British alliance had raided and destroyed many American settlements over the past year. Washington planned to put a stop to that.

Caroline and Nathan were not selected to join this expedition. Instead, they remained in their encampment at New Windsor on the edge of the Hudson River. Today, however, Nathan had been called away to a special meeting, one Caroline was not invited to. It was probably a mission or new offensive.

"I don't understand." Caroline sulked while washing her clothes, wondering why she was excluded. "I'm as good a shot as any. It shouldn't matter if I'm a woman or not."

While wearing a robe, she wrung out her shirt and took it over to a clothesline for it to dry in the hot sun. When she turned around, Nathan was headed her way.

"You got room on the line for one more?" He unbuttoned his shirt.

"I suppose." She took it and began washing it, waiting for him to share what news he had. When he didn't, she looked up at him. "Well?"

"Well—" Nathan hesitated. "They're planning a raid on the outpost at Stony Point down by the river."

"Stony Point." Caroline's brows rose. "The last we heard there were still thousands of Redcoats there. That's hard terrain to traverse. How are we going to retake it?"

"The latest intelligence said that most of the Redcoats have moved farther south. There are several hundred British left at Stony Point, and Washington wants to take it back."

"When do we leave?" Caroline hung Nathan's washed shirt on the clothesline.

"We?" Nathan shook his head. "General Wayne has handpicked soldiers from different regiments for this mission."

"And what about me? I can shoot as good as anyone." Caroline's voice rose. "Where you go, I go—"

"Not this time." Nathan shook his head. "There will be little shooting in this battle. Knives and bayonets. Mostly hand-to-hand combat from what I understand."

"What?" She looked at him incredulously.

Nathan took a deep breath as uncertainty rose on his face. "We go in at night and wade across the marsh. If we make it that far, then we have to climb up the side of Stony Point—"

"Fighting in the dark with bayonets." Caroline's heart began racing as fear rushed in. "I don't want you to go!"

"There's no choice." Nathan looked down. "Can't say I'm too excited about this mission. If we don't catch them by surprise, there will be many of us not returning."

The tears rose as Caroline wrapped her arms around him, wishing someone else had been picked for the mission in his place. If only this hellish war could be over, and they could live their lives in peace.

That evening, Caroline sat by herself, looking up at the stars of summer. Though every battle had its risk, the one that lay before Nathan troubled Caroline to no end. The decision by General Washington to retake Stony Point seemed reckless, especially when it involved her husband.

"This is why I should never have gotten married," she whispered out loud. "At least not during a war."

Her attention turned to God as tears rose. "I've already lost everything. Please don't take my husband. I can't bear it."

"There you are." Nathan walked over and sat down beside her. "Beautiful night, isn't it?"

Caroline didn't reply. Right now, she battled her old nature, wanting to protect herself from further pain. But isolating herself from her love was wrong and pushing him away when he most needed her was hurtful. There was no balance to be found. This was the risk she agreed to when they exchanged their vows.

"I know what you're thinking—at least I believe I do." Nathan broke the silence. "I wish I could give you some kind of encouragement or guarantee that—"

"But you can't." Caroline wiped her tears. "No one can."

Nathan nodded and looked up into the sky. "Promise me this. No matter what happens to me in this battle, don't give up on your dream. Don't stop fighting for what is ours. For freedom."

Caroline's heart felt like it was breaking in two, and Nathan hadn't even left for battle. Could she continue the fight if he didn't return? Caroline pulled out the small flag Nathan had given to her and rubbed her thumb over the blue thread of fifty stars.

"I–I will try. . ."

"Well then, that's all any of us can do." He reached over, putting his hand in hers. "Isn't it?"

Caroline closed her eyes and sighed deeply, determined to let go of her fear and be strong for her husband. He needed the encouragement of a loving wife right now, not a crying little child afraid of losing everything. She leaned her head against Nathan's shoulder and allowed him to pull her close.

"I love you." He kissed her head. "And always will."

"And I love you." She squeezed him.

****

A few days later, Nathan kissed Caroline goodbye in the late afternoon and joined over 1,000 other soldiers for the night mission. A haunting emptiness filled Caroline's soul as he disappeared over the hill. This was the first time they had not fought side by side since Caroline joined the army.

"God, be with Nathan. Bring him home." Caroline fought tears as the emptiness grew within her soul. "Please!"

When midnight came, Caroline lay awake, unable to sleep. Unable to manage any kind of peace. Even now, she felt alone as if the love of her life was lost to the world. After tossing and turning, she finally fell asleep and into a dream.

A chill filled the stale air as Caroline strained to see in the darkness within the dream. Men cloaked under the cover of night quietly waded across a marsh, holding their rifles above their heads. Their destination: a steep hill leading upward to an armed outpost where a handful of torches burned.

"Nathan!" Caroline recognized her husband's profile in the moonlight.

— A PATRIOT'S DREAM —

If only he could hear her. If only she could fight beside him, watching his back.

Suddenly, British voices called out from above, and gunfire erupted. Musket balls whizzed through the air, ripping through the flesh of the American soldiers. The dead sank below the surface of the marsh while the living continued to push forward.

Nathan made it to the shore and quickly dashed uphill toward the occupied outpost. Caroline longed to help, but she was nothing more than a spectator.

"Be careful!" Caroline futilely called out to her husband.

When Nathan and his surviving comrades reached the top, they charged the British. Nathan blocked a stabbing lunge by a Redcoat and then ran him through with his bayonet. Another soldier stepped forward challenging Nathan. The two fell to the ground, wrestling for the upper hand. Nathan stabbed his enemy with a knife until the man's body went limp. As Nathan jumped to his feet, another Redcoat charged him.

"Nathan—watch out!" Caroline yelled.

The British soldier slammed the butt of his rifle into Nathan's forehead. As Nathan staggered, struggling to regain his balance, the Redcoat thrust his bayonet into Nathan's chest.

"Nooo!" Caroline screamed.

Nathan gasped and then collapsed to the ground. His body became still as blood flowed from the mortal wound. Caroline's heart felt like it had stopped while she helplessly looked on.

— A PATRIOT'S DREAM —

The Redcoat turned his gaze toward Caroline and stepped closer. The man's eyes glowed red as a sickly smirk grew on his face.

"He's dead. Now you're all alone, Caroline." The demonic-looking Redcoat mocked her in a deep, horrid tone. "All alone!" Haunting laughter flowed from his lips, growing louder by the moment.

Caroline screamed and jolted up from her sleep. Her whole body shook as fear saturated her soul.

"You are all alone now. . ." The dark voice reverberated in Caroline's head.

"No!" Caroline cried out, putting her hands over her ears.

She jumped up and ran outside into the darkness, unsure of where to go to escape the haunting chill of death that followed her.

"God—help me!" She sank to the ground and sobbed. "Help me. . ."

Dawn came hours later. Caroline sat by a creek with her knees bunched to her chest while rocking back and forth, seeking to comfort herself. The dream had been too realistic to be just a dream. The thing Caroline feared most had come to pass. Nathan was dead, and there was no one left in her life to love.

In the afternoon, the American soldiers returned to the encampment. Hundreds of Redcoats were among them, now prisoners of war. The mission had been a success but not without casualties.

— A PATRIOT'S DREAM —

"John." Caroline saw one of her comrades. "Where's Nathan?"

He shook his head. "I don't know. I haven't seen him since last night."

She ran alongside the returning soldiers, her eyes darting around, looking for her love, but he was nowhere in sight. When she reached the end of the troops, Caroline's broken heart began to bleed. How could she go on fighting for freedom now? Her strength and resolve had all but failed.

Caroline aimlessly walked through the camp until coming to an area of protruding rocks next to a stream. There Caroline wept, unable to comprehend that Nathan was gone. Unable to fathom that she was now alone in the world.

"Why, God?" Her chest shook with sobs. "Why?"

Promise me this. No matter what happens, don't give up on your dream. Don't stop fighting for what is ours. For freedom. Nathan's words from days earlier rose into her mind.

Caroline wiped her face as his words filled her heart. Could she do that now? Could she simply leave the past behind and press ahead? The sorrow and loneliness were overbearing.

She pulled out the flag Nathan had made and carefully studied it. God gave her the dream of the flag of fifty stars for a reason. It was as if Caroline had been charged by The Almighty to take hold of this dream and encourage others with it. Victory was theirs. All they had to do was not give up.

But giving up was all she wanted to do now. There was little left to live for. Still, Nathan's words continued to flow through her mind. Caroline closed her eyes, struggling to encourage herself.

Quitting would dishonor God and Nathan. She couldn't do that.

"Yes—" Caroline whispered as she sobbed. "I—I will grieve the loss of my husband and continue on in the fight—so help me God."

She clenched the flag in her fist, determined to honor her Maker. "Help me work past this pain so I can—"

Voices trickled in from behind. Caroline didn't want to be around others right now, much less talk to them. She needed to be by herself. After stuffing the flag back in her pocket, she quickly wiped her tears and rose, eyeing a place further down the creek.

"Caroline," a familiar voice called out.

She spun around, staring in disbelief. "Nathan?" Caroline's knees buckled, and she nearly collapsed.

Nathan stood some thirty feet away with the help of another soldier. A bloody bandage covered his forehead and another one around his thigh.

Caroline quickly gained her balance and ran toward him, praying this was not some kind of emotional delusion but real. She stopped and gazed into his eyes before lunging forward and embracing him.

"Careful." Nathan groaned in pain.

"How? I thought you were—" Caroline eased her hold on Nathan and looked back into his weary eyes. Before he could answer, a dam of emotions broke, and Caroline began sobbing.

"I got it from here," Nathan said to the soldier who had helped him.

As the man walked off, Nathan put his arms around Caroline who wept. He pulled back when the crying slowed, and gently wiped tears from Caroline's cheek. "I'm sorry you worried. I was slow at bringing up the rear with these blasted wounds."

The frayed nerves Caroline had suffered from began to meld back together. Her horrid dream seemed to have been nothing more than a ploy by the enemy of Caroline's soul to tear her apart with tormenting fear. Unfortunately, it had worked.

"I prayed but was so afraid for you." Caroline's voice quivered.

"The battle was fiercer than I thought it would be. Scariest moment of my life. I took a rifle butt to the head and got stabbed in the thigh." Nathan pulled up his shirt, revealing a bloody bandage around his abdomen. "I thought I was dead for sure. The Redcoat jabbed me with his bayonet, but it was as if his blade deflected off my chest, only clipping my side instead. Strangest thing. Guess it was not my time."

"God heard my prayers despite the fear." Caroline gently wrapped her arms around him, laying her head on his chest.

"That He did. I hope to never go through that again. Prefer a battle with a bit more distance from my enemy and a rifle filled with black powder and a musket ball." He sighed.

"Come on." Caroline gently slid her arm around Nathan, allowing him to put some of his weight on her. "Let's get you off your feet so you can rest."

The tears continued as they walked across the encampment, only these were no longer tears of sorrow and loss but joy and thankfulness. God had spared her husband and mended Caroline's broken heart.

— **A PATRIOT'S DREAM** —

— A PATRIOT'S DREAM —

Morristown, New Jersey
December 1779

"Those who expect to reap the blessings of freedom must, like men, undergo the fatigue of supporting it."
Thomas Paine

The hot summer came to an end, ushering in autumn. The month of November then quietly moved into December, and the air grew colder as winter came early.

Over two years had passed since Caroline joined the Continental Army. She had adjusted to living day to day, not knowing if life or death awaited her. Still, she dreamed of freedom and a life with Nathan, full of children, and grandchildren; a dream her parents had hoped for but never saw fully come to fruition.

Caroline marched ahead with Nathan and her comrades in arms. With winter upon them, the northern battles with the British had slowed, though the battles in the south raged on.

"I do believe it's colder now than the last two Decembers." Nathan rubbed his hands together.

"I'd rather battle those Redcoats in Georgia than sit around in the snow for another winter, freezing my britches off." Jordan, a soldier marching beside them, pulled his coat tight around his neck as the frigid breeze grew stiffer.

Caroline nodded in agreement. She preferred to fight and bring an end to this war than wait several months for winter to pass.

"How much farther do you think we have until we reach Morristown?" Caroline asked, feeling tired after several days of marching.

Nathan shrugged. "I've never been there before. Hopefully, not much longer."

"I was there three years ago right at the beginning of my service in the spring of '77." Jordan shifted his rifle to his other shoulder. "We'll have to build log barracks like we did at Valley Forge. Let's hope supplies are better this winter or we may not have much of an army left to face the British come spring. Regardless, I doubt I'll see any more action."

"What do you mean?" Caroline's brows rose.

"Come March, my three-year commitment is up. I'm going home."

"Home?" Caroline glanced over at Jordan in disbelief. "But what about the war?"

"I have a farm that's got to be attended to. My wife and youngins' have tried to keep it going but it's been quite a struggle for—"

"But you can't leave!" Caroline's voice rose. "We need you to—"

"Look, I fought as hard as I could and lived through it. I've seen my family only twice since I joined the army. *I'm going home.*"

Caroline understood but didn't understand at the same time. Maybe if her family was still alive, she might feel the same way.

Jordan was a good man and soldier whom she and Nathan had gotten to know better over the last several months. There were many half-hearted men whom she'd rather see leave the army instead of Jordan.

A day later they came to their campsite outside of Morristown, New Jersey, and immediately went to work cutting down trees. The reality of spending another winter in cold, dark barracks hit Caroline harder than she thought. Each day would seem like a week. Hopefully, there would be less snow during this winter.

The following day with a saw in hand, Caroline went to work trimming off the branches and limbs from the trees the men cut down.

Nathan walked by after cutting down another tree. "Hard to believe anyone could sweat this much with as cold as it is." He wiped his brow and drank from a canteen before handing it to Caroline.

She stood and rubbed her tired hands together. "I think we'll sleep well tonight." Caroline took the canteen and help it up to her mouth for a drink.

"We should." Nathan glanced up into the sky. "Oh, it looks like snow's coming. It's certainly bad timing."

Caroline handed the canteen back to Nathan and kissed him on the cheek. "Thank you, love."

Nathan glanced around and then leaned in, kissing her on the lips as light snow flurries began falling from the sky. "You're quite welcome."

Caroline smiled while warmth filled her soul. She loved this man with all her heart, God's gift to her in uncertain times. Where would she be now without his love, encouragement, and support?

By afternoon, the horses trudge through ankle-deep snow, hauling fallen trees out of the forest toward the encampment. Thanks to the inclement weather, the work of building the housing would now take longer.

****

Another Christmas came and went without much fanfare. Caroline and Nathan had no gifts to give other than their love for one another. Perhaps, this was how it would be for years to come as the war dragged on. Maybe Christmas would only be celebrated in the heart and never again with gifts, songs of hope and joy, or warm, savory food.

Caroline shivered as she carried wood toward her log barracks while the icy snow crunched under her worn boots.

This winter was proving to be much harsher than the years before; bitter cold and snow the Continental Army was not prepared for. Few had proper clothing, and food and supplies seemed even more scarce than during the winter at Valley Forge.

If the British were to wage an assault right now, would Caroline and her comrades have the strength or fortitude to fight? Every day, word spread of more soldiers deserting and going home. There seemed moments when Caroline held on to *the dream* of freedom by a thread.

She stopped briefly and looked up into the sky as the clouds parted and a ray of sunshine broke through.

"Oh, that feels good." Caroline closed her eyes, allowing the warmth of the sun to dance across her face.

There were times like this when, for but a moment, the weariness of war faded, and the glory of God seemed to fill her soul, infusing hope and strength.

"You are faithful," Caroline whispered. "You will do what you promised."

When she opened her eyes, Caroline noticed Nathan standing by the barrack's door, smiling.

"What?" Caroline smiled back.

"I love you," he said while walking over. "You look like an angel with that glorious sun shining on your face."

Caroline chuckled, knowing Nathan must be blinded by love. Her face was gaunt, and her body was dirty. How long ago had she bathed or eaten a good meal?

He kissed her and grabbed some of the wood from her arms as they headed inside the barracks occupied by ten other soldiers. Though the log structures kept most of the wind out, the cold still permeated in despite the fire. The damp chill of the barracks made Caroline long for the warmth of spring.

A week later during the night, Caroline awoke to a faint rustling sound. Jordan threw his pack over his shoulders along with his rifle and walked out the door of the barracks. It was clear he wasn't merely stepping out to relieve himself.

Caroline tore off her blanket, slid on her boots, and headed toward the door. After stepping outside, she caught sight of him in the moonlight.

"Jordan," she whispered loudly as she ran toward him. "Where are you going?"

He stopped and glanced around before looking at her with a perturbed expression on his face. "You need to go back to bed."

"You're leaving, aren't you?" Caroline's countenance dropped.

Jordan nodded.

"But you only have two months left before—"

"I'm likely to starve to death before March comes." He sighed. "Look, the odds of the British attacking during the winter are slim. Sitting around here with little food and warmth serves no purpose."

"But—"

"Caroline, I've fought a good fight. Now, my family needs me. Maybe once I've gotten things situated at home, I'll sign back up." He put his hand on her shoulder and smiled. "You are as fine a soldier as I've seen and carry more hope than most. Keep believing and don't give up."

— A PATRIOT'S DREAM —

A moment later, Jordan faded into the darkness as he headed back to his family in Virginia. Caroline's gaze fell to the frozen ground. Though only one man, Jordan was yet another setback in seeing *the dream* of freedom manifest.

She glanced up into the sky. "I know you see the beginning from the end." Caroline paused, unsure of how to shake loose the disappointment of constant setbacks. "I guess there's nothing more to do than stay the course and not give up."

With a heavy heart, Caroline sighed out loud and headed back toward the barracks.

****

The brutal cold continued into February while the number of those deserting the army climbed. The days seemed to slow to a snail's pace for Caroline with the main focus just trying to stay warm and ignore the groaning within her stomach. The last two months had felt like a year within this frozen hell. How she longed for Spring, even the sweltering heat of Summer.

Caroline woke abruptly in the early morning and quickly stepped out of the barracks holding her hand over her mouth. When she reached the latrine, she vomited what little food she had eaten the night before.

She stood and wiped her mouth with a handkerchief as beads of sweat rose on her forehead.

"What's wrong with me?" Caroline whispered as the nausea eased. "This is the fourth day in a row I've thrown up."

She started back toward her barracks while fear churned within her mind. Many had died of diseases within the camp. What kind of sickness had she contracted, and would it continue to grow worse and claim her life as it had others?

Caroline hadn't said anything to Nathan, not wanting to worry him while she hoped the sickness would go away. But what if it didn't?

With a heavy heart, Caroline stopped short of her barracks, struggling to hold back the tears. "Help me, God. Please heal me." She stepped inside and lay back down under the blanket feeling weak and tired.

There was no guarantee they'd be getting any food today. She rubbed her empty stomach. There were days they only got a little meat and other days a little bread. Two weeks ago, they went three full days without so much as a morsel of anything. How were they all going to make it through this? Victory seemed *so* far away. Perhaps, it was already out of reach.

"This is so dismal," Caroline whispered under her breath as she shivered. "Help us—please. Give me faith to keep believing."

She slowly drifted back to sleep. Within a dream, a breeze blew across her face, one not too hot or too cold. Her body no longer shivered in the bitter air of winter. Before her, the sun rose on the eastern horizon in hues of pink and purple.

"How glorious." Caroline breathed in deeply as she gazed upon the majestic colors of dawn.

A giggling sound filled the air, and Caroline glanced down. There within her arms was a small child of eighteen months with strawberry blonde hair and blue eyes.

"Isn't it lovely, Liza?" Caroline gently squeezed her little girl.

Though Caroline had never seen this child before, she somehow knew within this dream that Liza was her baby girl. She had named this child after Caroline's mother, Elizabeth, though Caroline preferred to call the child *Liza* for short.

Liza glanced up and pointed. "Look!"

Caroline followed the direction of Liza's finger. There above them, the flag of fifty stars fluttered in the morning breeze.

"How beautiful." Caroline's tears rose.

Liza turned and looked into Caroline's eyes, capturing her attention. Within the child's piercing gaze was an unnaturally great depth. It was as if Caroline was staring into the eyes of her Maker, receiving divine revelation. Without spoken words, Caroline knew victory was assured for her people. Her focus no longer needed to be on the harsh winter or lack of food.

Instead, her sight should be fixed on the unseen realm where provision for the body and soul abounded. God would give them what they needed. Freedom would follow.

— A PATRIOT'S DREAM —

Those beautiful blue eyes of her little girl slowly faded as the dream came to an end, though its essence remained, deposited within Caroline's spirit.

She felt a soft caress on her cheek and awoke. Nathan knelt beside her with a faint smile on his face.

"Good morning." His smile widened.

"Good morning." Caroline yawned, feeling surprisingly refreshed.

"You've slept late. Everyone is already up and about. Wish I had some food to offer, but I'm not sure what today holds."

Caroline nodded. "It's okay. We're going to make it."

"I like your optimism." He stood. "Well, I'm going to the latrine. I'll be back shortly." He kissed her on the cheek and left.

Caroline remained there under her blanket within the empty barracks as the dream rose back into her mind. "How odd I dreamed about a future child and even more so that I felt like I already knew her and—"

Suddenly, it became all too clear. Caroline glanced down at her stomach. She had missed the regularity of the last two months but hadn't thought much of it. Now she was sick—just like her mother had been when pregnant with Paul.

"I'm not dying—I'm pregnant!" Caroline whispered as her eyes widened.

She quickly sat up in shock. "But I can't be pregnant. Not now."

Caroline and Nathan had been careful when they were able to find time to be alone, trying to make sure this didn't happen. The last thing Caroline wanted to do was give birth to a child while they lived under British tyranny.

Still, the child's precious smile and sweet giggle filled Caroline's heart. "This baby is a child of freedom," she blurted out as she gently rubbed her stomach.

The door opened, and two of her comrades stepped inside, cursing the frigid weather. Caroline collected herself as the shock of being pregnant eased.

For now, she wouldn't say a word to anyone, lest they take her out of the army and not allow her to fight. No, this would be a secret between her and God until she could no longer hide it.

****

The frigid winter relentlessly moved into the month of March while food and supplies remained scarce. Many more had deserted the army while others were released from duty because of sickness or scant clothing which made them unfit to serve.

Despite it, Caroline continued to hold on to her faith, believing that victory lay before them at some point in the future. Giving up was no longer an option despite the many moments of discouragement.

At times, Caroline laughed to herself when thinking about the naive little fourteen-year-old girl she once was. That girl had signed on to fight the British, believing that victory was just around the corner. Sometimes she wondered if that fourteen-year-old had known what lay ahead would she have been just as enthusiastic about joining the army or would she have opted to stay with Aunt Mildred?

At the thought, Caroline shook her head. "No, I would have lost my mind living with that woman."

Caroline had been given a gift to see the future and speak of what she saw to others, encouraging them to believe in victory. It required her to walk by faith and not by sight as the Good Book said even when she didn't feel like it.

A large, outdoor fire crackled in the morning just after dawn, bringing greater warmth than the small fireplaces inside the dark barracks.

Standing in the ankle-deep snow, Caroline rubbed her hands together in front of the roaring fire before turning around and allowing her backside to warm up. Doctor Richardson, the man who had dressed Caroline's head wound after her first battle, stood with her, Nathan, and several other soldiers as they talked about past winters.

"When I was a boy back in the winter of '49, my brothers and I built a house of snow." The doctor smiled. "It was more like a fort."

"A house of snow?" Caroline's eyes widened. "How large was it?"

"Oh, not large. It was enough for the three of us to stand up inside it. Surprisingly, it was actually warmer inside than outside the fort. We were so proud of ourselves until the roof collapsed, followed by one of the walls. We then spent the rest of the day inside, drying our clothes out by the fire." He laughed.

"When I was a boy, two of my friends and I had a snowball fight. . ." Nathan smiled. "Inside the house. Mama walked in right after we'd finished. I'd never seen her that mad before. I cleaned up the mess but still got a whipping from Papa that night. Never did that again."

He turned to Caroline. "How about you? Did you have any fun in the snow?"

"One year, my papa helped Paul and I build a huge snowman. It was this wide." She stretched her arms out as far as she could. "Papa had to stand on—"

"Caroline. . ." Nathan cocked his head with a flat expression. "*Really?* That's pretty wide."

"Well." She grinned sheepishly. "Maybe it was really this size." The width of her arms narrowed slightly. "Anyway, Papa stood on a ladder to put—"

Just then, an officer ran up to them, nearly out of breath. "Redcoats have been spotted not two miles east of here. Grab your gear." He turned to Doctor Richardson. "Get your bag and join us."

Nathan's brows rose. "Is their entire army out there?"

The officer shook his head. "No, our scouts said it looks to be less than 100. Probably just spying on us. We need to keep them from returning to New York and reporting our situation."

Caroline, Nathan, and over a hundred of their comrades hurriedly marched eastward in the snow while more soldiers at the encampment were made ready to follow as reinforcements. This was the first battle Caroline could remember fighting in the intense cold and snow. Her nose ran while her cheeks burned in the frosty air. At least their quick pace would help keep their blood flowing.

After two miles of marching, the Americans slowed their gate and spread out into the forest. The only advantage to having the ground blanketed in white was that the red uniforms of the British would stand out more.

Caroline spotted tracks in the snow that appeared to be heading away from their position. She walked in silence with her eyes trained ahead and hands firmly wrapped around her rifle.

An eerie feeling rose up within her as if they were being watched, perhaps being led into an ambush. She glanced twenty feet away at Nathan who cautiously moved ahead, looking as if he sensed it too.

Suddenly, a Redcoat stepped out from behind a tree in the distance and fired. A small limb beside Caroline was sheared off by the shot. She quickly aimed and fired back before dodging behind a tree and pulling out another musket cartridge. The battle had begun.

Caroline could barely feel her fingers, slowing the process of reloading. This was one of many reasons why few battles were fought during the frigid winters.

She peered around the tree as the sound of gunfire erupted throughout the forest. The battle quickly grew in intensity. Caroline ran ahead and slid in the snow behind another tree. When a Redcoat stepped out to fire, she did the same, shooting the enemy in the shoulder.

The battle continued with the British slowly retreating.

After shooting, Caroline struggled to reload her rifle with numb fingers. She now longed to be back in the cold, damp barracks where at least she could feel her extremities. In another month or so, they would see the last of the cursed snow, something she relished the thought of.

When Caroline looked up, she froze. A Redcoat stood twenty feet away with his rifle trained on her. She had been careless, allowing her attention to be on her discomfort. Before she could take any action, the British soldier fired.

Caroline gasped out loud and doubled over as pain shot through her abdomen.

The Redcoat quickly tromped through the snow in her direction with his bayonet pointed at her. Caroline couldn't yell for help or move. At the last second, she lifted her rifle up and deflected the enemy's bayonet. The impact sent her hard to the ground. Caroline willed her body to move, but her strength had all but disappeared.

The British soldier kicked her rifle from her hands as he looked down at her with a scowl on his face.

"Bloody rebels." He spat on her. The man then raised his rifle, preparing to run her through with his bayonet.

"No!" Nathan yelled as he lowered his shoulder, ramming into the Redcoat.

The two slammed down into the snow and exchanged blows. As they fought, Caroline glanced to her right for her rifle and gasped. Her blood was staining the snow red. She refocused her attention on the weapon and wrapped her right hand around it. Caroline's rifle, however, felt heavy as lead.

— A PATRIOT'S DREAM —

With all the strength she could muster, Caroline lifted it out of the snow.

"Help me, God," she grunted as her hands trembled violently.

The British soldier had gotten the upper hand, pinning Nathan down while pulling out a dagger. Caroline struggled to fix the barrel of her rifle on the Redcoat. She pulled back the hammer with her thumb and then pulled the trigger. A musket ball exploded from her rifle and tore through her enemy's chest. The British soldier groaned and fell backward into the snow.

Nathan quickly crawled over to Caroline. Blood trickled down from a cut above his eye and on the corner of his mouth.

"Oh, God." A look of shock rose on his face. He quickly pressed his hand on her wound.

Caroline gasped. "That hurts!"

"We have to stop the bleeding. Where's the doctor?" Nathan's eyes darted around with a look of hopelessness. "I saw him just a moment ago—there!" He waved his hand. "Doctor Richardson! Over here! Hurry!"

The sound of crunching snow grew louder until the doctor was beside them.

"She's lost a lot of blood." Doctor Richardson knelt beside Caroline, examining the wound. His brows tightened. "There's too much blood to have come from this wound. Help me turn her over."

He and Nathan gently turned Caroline to her side while the doctor examined an apparent exit wound. She glanced back as Doctor Richardson's countenance fell. After laying her down on her back, he looked over at Nathan and shook his head.

Nathan grabbed the doctor's arm as he stood. "You've got to help her!"

"I'm sorry." Doctor Richardson put his hand on Nathan's. "The damage is too severe. With the amount of blood I see, it appears an artery was nicked. There's nothing I can do." He squeezed Nathan's hand. "I'm truly sorry."

"Doctor!" another soldier called out, needing help.

Doctor Richardson glanced over at Caroline with glassy eyes as sorrow filled his face. He quickly turned and ran off to help another of their comrades.

The look of hopelessness in the doctor's eyes sent a shiver down Caroline's spine. "I'm cold," her voice trembled.

Nathan tore off his coat and laid it across her.

As the reality of the moment hit, tears trickled down Caroline's face. "I—I thought I'd be alive to see freedom come to our country."

Nathan's eyes overflowed with tears while his lips quivered. There were no words of encouragement he could share, no hope to give her. Nathan's heart appeared to be ripping in two as life quickly flowed from Caroline's body.

The sight broke her own heart. She didn't have much time left and needed to be strong for her husband.

Caroline wiped her tears and reached into her coat pocket, struggling to pull out the Christmas gift from Nathan from the year they met. She opened her bloody hand, holding the stitched American flag with fifty stars, and glanced up at Nathan.

"This is your dream now. Take it and don't ever give up."

Nathan quickly wiped his face and put his hand in hers with the flag sandwiched between them. "I won't stop fighting until freedom is ours. I swear it."

"I know you will." The tears returned as Caroline gazed into the eyes of her husband. "I love you—with all my heart."

"And I—" a lump appeared to form in Nathan's throat, "—love you."

The white snow-covered forest dimmed as Caroline's time grew short. Then, the sun became brighter, only it wasn't the sun but a circle of light that widened.

"What is that?" She held up her hand, trying to touch it.

"I don't see anything." Nathan looked around.

The middle of the circle became translucent, revealing a figure.

"Papa!" Caroline smiled.

"What do you see, Caroline?" Nathan asked.

"I—I see my father and—" Caroline's eyes widened as more figures appeared. "Paul and Mama." There within her mother's arms was a small child with strawberry-blonde hair. "Liza!" Caroline's smile grew. "They're waiting for me."

The world around Caroline had become dark as the realm of heaven grew brighter. She turned to Nathan just able to make out his profile. With the last of her strength, she looked deeply into his face.

"Nathan—don't lose heart. Freedom *will* come."

Now Caroline could no longer see his face or hear his voice. She simply felt the squeeze of his hand. Then the world faded and the freedom of heaven enveloped Caroline. She was home.

****

Nathan looked on in disbelief as Caroline's last breath disappeared into the frigid air. Caroline's hand became limp within his, and her body grew still, though her eyes remained open, gazing up into the sky. She had passed on.

Loneliness instantly draped across Nathan's shoulders like a heavy shroud, crushing him. His heart felt like it had stopped beating.

"How can you be gone—" Nathan's voice quivered. "How. . ."

He laid his head on Caroline's chest and began weeping as his will to live wavered.

Agonizing moments passed while sorrow and darkness swirled around him. If only it could have been Nathan who died so that Caroline could have experienced the freedom she had dreamed of. The pain of loss became too great for him to manage. If he could join her now in death, he would gladly do so.

— A PATRIOT'S DREAM —

Within the darkness, a crystal clear vision suddenly filled Nathan's eyes. Caroline stood at the base of a pole, one surrounded by hundreds of others—maybe thousands. These were all who had passed on during their fight for freedom. Above them on the pole, a banner of red, white, and blue fluttered in the wind. Within the blue of the flag, fifty stars glowed as if made of light. He gasped at the vision, one that felt as real as the world around him.

"I see it, Caroline!" he whispered in amazement. "The same flag you had in your dreams."

Suddenly, vigor and life began flowing through Nathan's spiritual veins, infusing him with fire and the strength to go on. He sat up and opened his hand, looking at the small flag with Caroline's blood on it. The gift he gave her to instill hope would now be a reminder to him of where their hope could truly be found.

Nathan lifted his head, wiped his eyes, and looked up into the sky. "I vow to give myself to Your service to see freedom come. I will never stop until it does. . . so help me, God."

He leaned over and kissed Caroline on the forehead. Nathan then gently caressed her cheek while looking into those hazel-green eyes once more. The memories of the first day he had met her flooded Nathan's mind. What a great encouragement and gift she had been to him. It was a gift that he now had to return to his Maker. Nathan would carry on the flame of passion that once burned in Caroline's heart.

"Goodbye, Caroline," Nathan spoke with tearful affection. He then moved his hand over her face and gently closed her eyes. "I *will* see you again one day, my love."

— A PATRIOT'S DREAM —

Yorktown, Virginia
October 1781

"The harder the conflict, the more glorious the triumph."
Thomas Paine

Nathan yelled as he and his comrades charged with their bayonets toward the enemy. Several grenades went off around them and shots whizzed through the air, but the Americans didn't stop their assault.

A great opportunity now lay before the Continental Army. General Washington had cornered British General Cornwallis's army onto the peninsula of Yorktown. Word of British reinforcements from New York coming to aid the general only propelled the Americans and French to push even harder against their enemy before that could happen.

— A PATRIOT'S DREAM —

After driving his bayonet through a Redcoat, Nathan continued on with great veracity. The small battle raged on until the British garrison surrendered.

With more ground taken, General Washington moved the cannons closer to the British forces and opened fire. All day long, the Americans and French fired artillery at Cornwallis's army. There was nowhere left for their enemy to go.

The following morning, Nathan sat on an embankment, watching the sun rise while the allied American and French forces continued shelling the British position. Despite having finished his three-year commitment with the Continental Army, Nathan stayed on. He promised Caroline and made an oath to God that he would not stop fighting until freedom came, and he intended to fulfill that.

Many scars covered his body from being shot, stabbed, and even burned, but God had protected him from death.

In the midst of the exploding artillery, Nathan heard something. He stood to his feet with his rifle in hand and gazed out into the distance. A British drummer was banging on a large drum while an officer behind him began waving a white flag.

Nathan held his breath, wondering if this surrender was real or a trick. General Washington soon called for a halt to the shelling. A chill ran down Nathan's spine as they led the British officer across enemy lines to the American side for possible interrogation.

"Could this be it?" Nathan whispered to himself. "The moment we've been dreaming of—praying for?"

— A PATRIOT'S DREAM —

The following day, it became official. General Cornwallis and his entire army had surrendered. Nathan and a contingent of American troops flooded the British encampment in Yorktown, taking thousands of Redcoats prisoner. This would indeed cripple the British army and undoubtedly bring an end to the war sooner than later.

As their defeated enemy marched toward a prison camp, tears filled Nathan's eyes. "If only you could be here, Caroline," he whispered, wishing she could hear him. "What a glorious sight this would be for you, my love."

With a bulk of the British army now prisoners of war, no major battles ensued. Only skirmishes here and there. Several months later, the British parliament past a resolution, bringing an end to the war. Then in September of 1783, the Treaty of Paris was signed, and the American colonies were officially a sovereign nation of states. Freedom had come but at a great cost.

****

Nathan walked over to the ledge of a mountain in North Carolina and looked out on the western horizon. His people called this mountain Black Dome while the Cherokees called it Attakulla. It was said to be the tallest mountain within The Colonies.

This morning, pockets of fog settled into the valleys below while a golden sun rose overhead. Nathan closed his eyes and breathed in deeply of the morning air as a cool, refreshing wind blew over the summit.

— A PATRIOT'S DREAM —

He opened his eyes. "God, this is so beautiful."

The hike up to the summit over the past two days had been like a healing balm, washing over the blood, trauma, and death in battle that he had experienced during the last several years. War had stolen his innocence and nearly taken his life. The boy of seventeen was no more. Now he was a man full of hope though still battling brokenness.

With the war finally over, the American Colonies were now the American States, a united people free of tyranny and oppression.

How many lives had been lost in the fight to achieve this? Caroline had been but one of the thousands of casualties, yet her death had stolen part of his heart, a piece that could never be retrieved or replaced.

"There is so much work ahead to rebuild that which has been destroyed. I have a feeling that it will be hard and messy before it becomes a great light of freedom to the world."

"What should I do, my love?" Nathan sighed as he thought of Caroline. "I struggle to find my place in this new republic."

His gaze remained toward the west. Caroline had once said that within a dream, she had stood on the summit of a tall mountain well to the west of The Colonies. It had inspired her all the more to hope and believe in freedom.

"Maybe if the Lord is willing, I'll seek out that wondrous mountain, follow in your footsteps to the top, and dare to dream of the possibilities within this newfound freedom."

— A PATRIOT'S DREAM —

"We have this day restored the Sovereign to Whom all men ought to be obedient. He reigns in heaven and from the rising to the setting of the sun, let His kingdom come."
Samuel Adams